Her life ha

And it wasn't over yet. She'd married her partner, Nick, and gotten pregnant. She, who had never even played with dolls, had discovered a maternal streak a mile wide. She'd even talked the legendary Nick Whittaker into quitting the CIA with her to make sure their baby would have a real storybook family, something neither of them had ever had.

Then everything fell apart.

Catching sight of her fists, Reese opened them slowly and stared at the clever hands that went with the body and brains she'd used to build her own legend with the U.S. Marines and the CIA. It was time to see justice done, even if it meant going back to the life she'd thought she'd left behind....

Dear Reader,

We're thrilled to bring you another exhilarating month of captivating women and explosive action! Our Bombshell heroines will take you for the ride of your life as they come under fire from all directions. With lives at stake and emotions on edge, these women stand and deliver memorable stories that will keep you riveted from cover to cover.

When the going gets tough, feisty Stella Valocchi gets going, in *Stella, Get Your Gun,* by Nancy Bartholomew. Her boyfriend's a lying rat, her uncle's been murdered and her sexy ex is back in town, but trust Stella—compared to last week, things are looking up….

Loyal CIA agent Samantha St. John has been locked up—for treason! With the reluctant help of her wary partner, Sam will hunt for the real traitor—who bears an uncanny resemblance to Sam herself—in *Double-Cross,* by Meredith Fletcher, the latest adventure in the twelve-book ATHENA FORCE continuity series.

Don't miss the twists and turns as a former operative is sucked back into the spy life to right the wrongs done to her family, in author Natalie Dunbar's exciting thriller, *Private Agenda.*

And finally, a secret agent needs a break—but when her final mission goes wrong, she's pushed to the limit and has to take on a rookie partner. Luckily she's still got her deadliest weapon… it's *Killer Instinct,* by Cindy Dees.

When it comes to excitement, we're pulling no punches! Please send me your comments c/o Silhouette Books, 233 Broadway, Suite 1001, New York, NY 10279.

Sincerely,

Natashya Wilson
Associate Senior Editor, Silhouette Bombshell

Please address questions and book requests to:
Silhouette Reader Service
U.S.: 3010 Walden Ave., P.O. Box 1325, Buffalo, NY 14269
Canadian: P.O. Box 609, Fort Erie, Ont. L2A 5X3

PRIVATE AGENDA

NATALIE DUNBAR

Silhouette®

BOMBSHELL™

Published by Silhouette Books

America's Publisher of Contemporary Romance

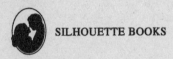

SILHOUETTE BOOKS

ISBN 0-373-51329-1

PRIVATE AGENDA

Copyright © 2004 by Natalie Dunbar

This edition published by arrangement with Harlequin Books S.A.

® and TM are trademarks of Harlequin Books S.A., used under license.
Trademarks indicated with ® are registered in the United States Patent
and Trademark Office, the Canadian Trade Marks Office and in other
countries.

Visit Silhouette Books at www.eHarlequin.com

Printed in U.S.A.

NATALIE DUNBAR

believes that a woman can do anything she sets her mind to. To date she has met her personal goals of becoming an electrical engineer working in the field, obtaining her master's degree in business administration and getting published. Happily married to her high school sweetheart, she lives in the Detroit area with him and their two boys. She has several romance novels under her belt, and is ecstatic over the launch of Silhouette Bombshell, which gives her characters new worlds to conquer. An avid fan of fiction, television and movies that showcase powerful women with strong skills and talents in a male-dominated world, she is happy to add her heroine, CIA agent Reese Whittaker, to the list.

This book is dedicated to all the real bombshell women of the world who save lives, serve their country and humankind, protect the innocent and benefit the world with the unique combination of strength, talent, intelligence and intuition known only to women.

Acknowledgments

As always, thanks to God for making it all happen. Thanks to Mavis Allen for referring my work to Julie Barrett. Thanks to my wonderful editor, Julie Barrett, for buying the manuscript and working with me to make this book the best it could be. Heartfelt and sincere thanks to Randy Stevens and Terry Lassaline for critiquing, reality checks and flavor. Thanks to my fantastic critique group, Reon Laudat and Karen White-Owens for quick and thorough reads, valuable input and moral support. Thanks to Vincent Murry for listening and giving me his two cents' worth. Lots of love and thanks to my family for all their love, patience and support while I worked on this book.
I appreciate you all.

Prologue

Squinting against the March afternoon sun, Reese Whittaker crossed the cream-colored carpeting and took a seat on the flowered sofa. *Relax. Now.* She pressed her ramrod-straight back against the stuffed pillows and tried to smooth the grimace of her lips into something less alarming. It didn't help to see the picture on the wall of herself at twelve, with a ten-year-old Riley sporting a short marine haircut. Her throat closed. It wasn't right that everything should look so normal, as if her beloved baby brother might come home from work any minute.

Forcing her gaze away from the picture, she allowed herself a few moments of self-pity. The past year of her life had been pure hell and it wasn't over yet. She'd married Nick and gotten pregnant. She, who had never even played with dolls, had discovered a maternal streak a mile wide. She'd even talked the legendary Nick Whittaker into quitting the CIA with her to make sure the baby would have a real, storybook family, something neither of them had had. Then everything fell apart.

Catching sight of her fists, Reese opened them slowly and flexed her fingers, staring at the clever hands that went with the body and brains she'd used to build her own legend with the marines and the CIA. This body that had also won her track and field and martial arts awards, had failed to hold on to one precious little baby. And in the midst of the most personal battle of her life, Nick Whittaker had proven that he didn't love her enough when he accepted a dangerous assignment. Alone she had fought to keep their child growing inside her.

In the background, she heard Riley's wife Carol calling little Candace. By the time the child reached the living room, Reese had a smile pasted on.

"Aunty Ree!" Six-year-old Candace climbed onto Reese's lap to kiss her cheek. "I missed you, Aunty Ree."

"I missed you too, sugar." She hugged the child's small body close to hers.

Her niece regarded her with large, golden-brown eyes full of innocence. "Aunty Ree, have you seen my daddy?"

"No, Candy." Forcing the words from a throat so tight she could barely breathe, Reese almost shook with the effort it took to keep the knowledge out of her expression. Somehow she managed to swallow.

Riley had been providing his antiterrorism and security expertise to the embassy in Rwanda. It had been bombed two days ago. His body had not been among the charred remains, so she'd been holding on to hope while the investigation continued. That hope waned as time went on. Soon, someone from the U.S. government would be telling Carol her husband was missing in action and presumed dead.

Reese smoothed one of Candy's chocolate-colored braids. Today she'd heard a rumor that the CIA knew who was responsible for the bombing, but was holding back on an arrest for other reasons. She meant to get to the bottom of that rumor and shake things up, even if it meant going back to work for the CIA.

In the name of justice, someone was going to pay for what had happened to her brother.

Chapter 1

In a deep funk after completing her "team" requalifications, Reese sat at her CIA desk trying to plan her next move. She'd suffered from gestational hypertension and preeclampsia during her six-month pregnancy, which caused her precious daughter Nicole to be stillborn and left her forty pounds heavier. With her crash diet and training program, she'd narrowly met the agency weight requirement, but in typical fashion she'd aced the physical test. Flaherty, her section chief, had been glad to get one of his best agents back.

Both feet rested on the gray desk as she stared

at her monitor and tapped a finger on the keyboard. One week in the office after eight months away and, except for Nick's absence, it was like she'd never left. She'd set up her new office and gotten reacquainted with the team. She'd also checked open agency and source files for information on the Rwandan embassy bombing, piecing together the evidence and confirming some rumors. Riley's body was still missing, but presumed burned to ash.

In a weak moment she'd even analyzed agency files against the info Flaherty had given her two days ago when he'd sent an extraction team to rescue Nick and the missionaries from the Colombian rebel camp where they'd been imprisoned. She found nothing new. That bothered her. There should have been an update from the extraction team.

Her restless fingers closed on a pencil, moving up and down yellow-painted wood. That moment when she'd held little Nicole's body in the hospital, knowing that her beautiful baby would never open her eyes, still haunted her. The pencil snapped in her fingers. Dammit, Nick should have been there. Or did it bother her more that it had been one of the few times in her life when her strength had failed her?

Leaning over, she tossed the broken pencil into the trash. She expelled her pent-up breath on a sigh. She'd filed papers to 'divorce Nick for not being the husband she thought he should be, but she didn't want anything to happen to him. Lord help her, he didn't even know about Nicole.

A message popped up on her screen in large red letters: MISSION BRIEFING AT 1400 HOURS. Flaherty was back. Swinging her legs off the desk, she stood, shut off the laptop and retrieved her PDA. Then she headed for the briefing room.

The mere thought of a new mission usually got her juices flowing, but this time she had too many other things on her mind. Gritting her teeth and rotating her shoulders, Reese tried to loosen up. Whatever this mission was, she didn't want it, especially now that she had a name and a face for the SOB who'd provided the weapons and explosives for the Rwandan embassy bombing. If Nick was in the hands of the extraction team, going after her brother's killer topped her list. The reality was that refusing a mission was not an option and being back with the CIA meant doing the assignments they gave her.

With each step of her boots up the black-and-gold marble corridor, four gritty years of training kicked in. She'd already begun the mental preparation for the upcoming mission. This time she knew she could depend only on herself.

Stepping into Briefing Room 2, Reese blinked against the bright lights mounted in the ceiling tiles. In a rumpled gray suit and a Superman tie, Evan Flaherty stood in a corner, loading a CD into the media system. The brilliant light failed to flatter his thick, brownish blond hair or his fair complexion. Steel-gray eyes lit up at the sight of her, his mouth forming a smile beneath his bushy moustache.

"Welcome back, Reese. You look good."

"Surprised?" she asked, thinking about the weight she'd been carrying when she'd gone out on maternity leave. Built tall and solid, she would never be skinny, but now she was a size twelve again.

She'd kept the bigger breasts pregnancy had brought her and skipped cutting the dark-brown curls that now hung close to her shoulders. She wore no foundation on her flawless skin, but she'd used eyebrow pencil and liner on her golden brown eyes, and added a rich wine-colored lipstick to her full lips. Now she felt like the lethal beauty Nick had nicknamed her.

Flaherty shook his head. "No, I'm not surprised, but you still deserve the compliment."

Nodding, she acknowledged the praise. "You look the same." Placing her pocket PC on one of the modular gray desks, she switched on its media panel and computer and made an attempt at small talk. "How's Rita?"

His smile widened and his eyes softened the way they always did when he talked about his wife. "Anxious to go on vacation to New Zealand, but I'd just as soon go somewhere tropical and closer."

The corners of Reese's mouth lifted in amusement. She could just imagine Flaherty and his wife enjoying themselves in Florida. It looked something like the last vacation she'd taken with Nick. The memories made her body tingle.

Straightening her back and rubbing her hands together, she made the smile disappear. She had to quit thinking about Nick. He'd made his choice and it wasn't her. Reese bit her lip.

"Coffee?" she mumbled, determined to think of something else.

"On the sideboard." Flaherty gave her one long, knowing look and then went back to loading the mission data.

Reese straightened her shoulders. The man saw too much. Working together for four years, they'd formed a relationship that had served them well. She'd begun with various partners, but once Flaherty paired her with Nick, they'd become his miracle team. Flaherty had always held up his end, even when it wasn't politically correct.

Flaherty closed the media panel and joined her at the sideboard. "You've had some tough breaks. I know that work is the best thing for you right now—but are you sure you're up to this?"

Pouring coffee into a foam cup and stirring in artificial sweetener, Reese Whittaker bristled at the question. "What is this, Evan? You guys don't pay agents to sit around the office."

"You are one of our best agents, but a lot has happened," Flaherty said, justifying himself, "I have to know that you're fit for duty."

"I'm fine. What's the latest on Nick?" she asked, seizing the opportunity and suppressing a flash of pain. "He should have been out by now."

Flaherty answered in even tones, his eyes assessing her. "We're still working on getting him out, but the situation has improved drastically. I'm expecting something to break any minute."

Reese felt relief wash over her. Flaherty wasn't giving her any specifics, but it sounded like Nick would be okay. She lifted the steaming cup to her lips with both hands, willing them to be steady.

"When they check in," Flaherty added, "I could arrange for you to talk to him for a few minutes."

Her throat tightened at the thought. Strung out alone on the naked edge of grief and depression, she'd finally realized that Nick was married to his job and the thrills it provided. She'd filed for divorce to close that chapter of her life. Now that she was thinking more rationally, she wasn't about to let Nick talk her out of it.

But he had been looking forward to Nicole's birth. She would have to tell him about the baby.

She gulped down hot coffee, letting it free her throat. "Thank you, Evan. I'd appreciate that."

Eyes gleaming approval, Evan slung one arm around her shoulders in an awkward hug.

She lifted her head and spoke confidently. "I've got my edge back and I'm fit for duty. Let's talk about the mission."

Dropping his arm, he said, "I selected you for this one because of your weapons expertise and successful track record, but there's an added opportunity that only you would appreciate. After all you and Nick have accomplished for us, I think I owe you this. All I ask is that you keep your focus on the primary mission at all times."

"Of course." Studying his face, her mind raced ahead, trying to make sense of his cryptic words.

"You're going to have to gain their trust, so you may be undercover for several months."

Reese nodded. Except for her vow to ensure justice for her brother, it sounded like just what she needed. "Details?"

Checking the doorway, he beckoned and called out, "Larry, over here."

A fresh-faced, sandy-haired young man in blue chinos and a matching print sport shirt entered the room and quickly strode toward them with youthful enthusiasm.

With a start, Reese remembered something she'd thrust to the back of her thoughts. *They'd never sent her anywhere without a partner.* Behind a neutral expression, Reese's hackles rose. If this was her new partner, she hoped he could take care of himself. Before Nick, she'd lost two partners despite their expertise and precautions. Each loss had deeply affected her.

She'd lost her first partner, Fred, when their plane was shot down on a nuclear weapons intelligence-gathering mission in North Korea. With a head wound from the onboard explosion, he hit the water tangled in his parachute and drowned. Despite a broken arm and metal shards in her side, Reese had pulled him from the depths and tried to revive him. Her second partner, Ben, was caught, interrogated, and killed mere seconds before she arrived to rescue him from a terrorist cell in Toronto. Still, she'd managed to capture the head of one of the most virulent terrorist groups threatening the security of the United States. Third in line, Nick Whittaker had successfully completed the mission with her.

Now, in a trademark blend of warmth and professionalism, Flaherty made introductions. Reese listened closely to the details he added on Larry's background. "Reese, meet Larry Hammond, MIT grad in systems and electrical engineering, and one of the best electronic security systems design and computer experts. He's been with the FBI two years, is a judo expert, and your partner for this joint CIA/FBI assignment."

"Larry."

Admiration shone in Larry's eyes. "I've been looking forward to meeting you because you're something of a legend here," he said.

Reese's lips curved upward. Score one for youthful enthusiasm.

"Larry, meet Reese Whittaker, Naval Academy grad, computer science and cryptography. Expertise in systems analysis, software engineering, judo and tae kwon do, and weaponry, one of our best agents, former marine. And your new partner," Flaherty added with a touch of pride.

Shaking hands with Larry, Reese noted that with the two-inch heels on her boots, they were the same height, six feet. His grip was firm and professional, though his enthusiastic energy made her want to dismiss the intelligence and curiosity in his green eyes. But she wasn't so naive as to judge him on appearance alone.

Flaherty waited until they'd both settled into their briefing modules with computers and media screens up and running. Then he turned to the media board and fingered the remote. A satellite picture filled the screen.

"Detailed government reports of geographical areas, military installations, troop movements and positions, and other image-based intelligence rely on information provided by our Key Hole–class satellites. They orbit the earth and provide images via electronic link with resolutions as fine as ten to fifteen centimeters."

The screen morphed into the next slide: a slim, pale, dark-haired man with a big forehead and thick glasses. He looked like a computer geek.

"This is Dr. Jess Conover, who developed the

new decipher code for the government Key Hole satellites after the previous code was compromised. This code provides access to all Key Hole information and was to be approved by the National Security Agency. It was stored on a compact disk that was stolen from a government facility in Los Angeles three days ago during a live test. Conover was killed. Without Conover to alter the code to enable copying, all we have is what's on the satellites and the disk. We can't use our own code, and it takes a year or more to develop a new one. The good news is that it also will take time for anyone else to decipher the code. Your mission is to locate and retrieve the disk."

Reese sipped her coffee and waited for the rest. The agency obviously had a major lead. Why else would they be sending her undercover?

The screen showed a handsome man with a charming smile. Blue-green eyes and a rugged face vaguely resembling Brad Pitt's complemented hair that was a natural blend of dishwater brown to white blond.

Temperature rising, Reese stared, not sure what to think. She'd accessed that face in the files. It was the man who'd provided guns and explosives for the embassy bombing. Eyes narrowed through a haze of anger and bewilderment,

Reese gripped the arms of her chair. The agency had proof that Barkley was responsible. Why hadn't they gone after him? She'd been waiting to ask Flaherty that one. Damn if she was going to let Barkley get away with it.

Flaherty studied her carefully, missing nothing. "Kevin Barkley. We've just had an informant connect him to the code theft. Our source has also learned that Barkley is involved with illegal weapons and training of mercenaries for hire for terrorist operations. Problem is, we don't have enough proof. Once you retrieve the disk, we'll bust Barkley with the evidence and close him down."

Reese studied the screen, making a quick summary of the situation. *They haven't busted Barkley for Rwanda because of the code disk. Get that disk and get Barkley.*

Flaherty continued. "Barkley's moneymaker is a successful post-9/11 paramilitary and survival training facility outside of Grayling, Michigan, with connections to facilities in other countries. It caters to people concerned about homeland invasion. The legitimate activities include martial arts, gun safety, and training for weapons on the ATF-approved list." He paused to drink some of his coffee.

"Based on the story we planted with Barkley, our contact knows you from the work you did with a group of marines busted for dealing drugs and selling government weapons and explosives."

While Reese digested this, Flaherty flashed pictures of a large facility with a guarded gate, set on several acres of private land. "The facility has evolved into a paramilitary community with about two hundred people including guards, service staff, dining facility, barracks, gym and instruc-tors in military science. Even now, they're in the process of constructing new buildings."

Flaherty turned away from the screen. "The lab is working on a device to verify the code disk. Reese, you'll reach the facility first and teach small-arms basics."

She shot him a questioning glance. She wanted this mission but she had to know the parameters. "No issues with race or FBI jurisdiction?"

"No." Flaherty shook his head. "This place is not like some of the militia groups that have existed in Michigan. Barkley is motivated by military operations and training and money, not some white supremacist agenda. You'll fit right in. And because of your weapons knowledge and undercover work, the interagency Homeland Security commission wants you for the job."

At Reese's nod, he continued. "The story is that you escaped prosecution, but were less than honorably discharged. You're laying low, waiting for the next big opportunity. We deleted records that would raise a flag with Barkley and got a special recommendation from his mentor in the Marines."

Flaherty gave her a thick envelope. "A brief on your mission and background story, all we could get on the other instructors at the camp, and more intel... Read and memorize the code phrases and the extraction points."

"What about Larry?" Reese asked.

"He'll start a few days later. They hire ex-cons and locals to cook and do menial tasks. Larry will be an ex–gang member on parole. He'll cook in the mess hall. Larry's a chameleon and can fit in anywhere." Flaherty gave Larry a thick white envelope too. "Read and memorize."

Larry and Reese studied the contents. Reese stopped at a photo of a striking man, Arturo Bodega. Something about him intrigued her. He had dark, deep-set eyes, chiseled cheekbones and beautiful bronze-colored skin. A former member of the Brazilian Special Forces, he taught martial arts classes at the facility.

Rob Morrison, in the next picture, was pasty

white with midnight-black hair and pale blue eyes. The dossier said he'd arrived at the Barkley Specialized Training Facility in search of his brother. He'd stayed. It didn't say whether Morrison had found him.

Reese wondered what Lana Fields, the buxom, blue-eyed blonde in the next picture, was doing at the facility. Skilled with knives and having done hard time for using one to kill her husband, Lana taught classes on self-defense.

Drew Walters, the creep in the next file, with small gray eyes, large nose and thin lips, had done prison time for multiple rapes and had beaten one woman into a coma. A security systems expert, he was paranoid and dangerous.

Paging through the rest of the files, she knew this assignment would be no picnic. Most of Barkley's instructors were graduates of the government and military prison systems and were people who'd displayed little respect for human life. Three had been court-martialed and had spent time in Leavenworth. There was even an ex-FBI agent in the group. But all this meant little when pitted against the opportunity to nab Barkley. Reese was virtually smiling at her luck.

Flaherty shut off the media screen. "The word is out that the code will be offered at an international auction in three months. We suspect he already has a buyer. We cannot allow this code to get into enemy hands. Your *first* priority is the code disk. *Then* you can bring Barkley in."

Since when did Flaherty have to remind her of her priorities? And what about the emphasis on bringing Barkley in? She saw knowledge in the eyes gazing back at her. *He knew she'd gotten the intel on Barkley and Rwanda.*

Her fingers gripped the pen so hard that it bent. "First priority, the code disk," Reese repeated.

Flaherty handed her a small box. Reese opened it to find gold, disk-shaped earrings set with semi-precious stones. "These are nice. What do they do?"

"They're Charge Coupled Device technology video cameras," Flaherty said, proudly pointing to the screen where Reese was pictured.

"Hey!" Reese fiddled with the screw that locked the earring onto her ear. The cameras zoomed in. She examined the earrings, knowing there was a hidden silicon-imaging sensor with a tiny array of light-sensitive diodes beneath the stones.

She would have to sit near the window at her meetings so that images could be beamed to a sensor planted outside, then compressed, encrypted and beamed to the agency through a communications satellite.

Flaherty also gave her the miniature recorder and battery cable.

"What about my communications link?" she asked.

"Your communications link." Flaherty produced small plastic bags, each containing a tiny device. "This time we have an implant that's virtually undetectable. We'll broadcast my encrypted signal into the camp when needed, and listen in on your meetings with Barkley through the comm link. We hear everything you hear and say. You'll hear us in your ear. You'll be able to turn it off for privacy."

With that, Flaherty ended the briefing.

As Larry headed for the lab, Flaherty got the call from the extraction team in Colombia and asked Reese to come into his office.

Mentally preparing herself, Reese was silent. She had to tell Nick the news. She owed him that much. Inadequate words cycled in her head. Her armpits were damp, her hands icy cold.

Flaherty was breaking the rules by letting her talk to Nick before he'd been debriefed. When he got Nick on the line, he faded into a corner of the room.

Reese curved her fingers around the receiver and lifted it to her ear. "Nick?"

"Reese! Oh, I've been dying to hear your voice. I missed you." Nick sounded weary but relieved. "Talk to me, sweetheart."

She let the familiar sound of his deep voice wash over her for a minute. "How are you?"

"Sick, but it's nothing serious. I've got a doctor taking care of me and I'm coming home soon." His breathing was raspy. "I want to know how you are."

"I'm...okay." She struggled to keep from shaking.

His voice took on an edgy note. "I don't have to see your face to know that's a lie." When she didn't respond, his voice softened. "Tell me about the baby. I bet she has your eyes."

It took two tries to clear her throat. "She's gone."

"What do you mean?" The words were harsh with disbelief.

Her throat tight with emotion, Reese broke the stark silence that followed his words. "Nicole was stillborn."

"No! Sweet Mary, mother of Jesus, no!" His voice was raw with grief and sorrow. "Reese..."

Her eyes closed and her chest so heavy that she

found it hard to breathe, the words came in a rush. "The hypertension got worse and I developed preeclampsia. It ravaged my kidneys and the placenta and took Nicole's life.... I can't stop seeing her little face."

"Ree, I wish... If things had gone the way I planned—" Nick's voice shook, and she knew he was trying to be careful with her feelings and struggling with his own. "I should have been with you."

"Yes, you should have." Hurt and anger fed into her voice, raising the volume and sharpening the pitch. "When it happened, I blamed you for abandoning us."

Nick's voice went uncharacteristically hoarse. "You know damn well it wasn't like that."

A blend of grief, anger and pain poured from her, making her next words cut like glass. "And you didn't get a thrill out there playing hero while I was here going through hell?"

Nick was silent for several moments. Then she heard his voice again, this time low and vibrating with emotion.

"If I had known that things were that bad, I would have stayed home with you. Reese, I love you."

She didn't say she loved him, too. Instead, she

pushed for more. "You didn't answer the question."

Now anger crept into Nick's voice. "Did I get a thrill? What do you want me to say? Hell, yes, I got a thrill! You would have too. That's why we both chose this job."

Her nose was running from unshed tears. "I had made a vow to leave that life behind. I—I've filed for divorce, Nick. Now I just think we should spend some time apart and—and see how it goes."

"Reese, we need each other now. It's not like you to cut me off like this. Don't you feel anything for me?"

She grabbed a tissue from the box on Flaherty's desk and pressed it to her teary eyes. "Yeah, but right now, most of it is pretty negative."

"Let me make it up to you. Let me talk to you." A note of pleading that affected her more than she wanted to admit crept into Nick's normally confident voice.

Reese reined in her emotions, making her voice ring with strength. "No, Nick. I think we made a mistake getting married. I'm glad you're back and going to be okay. You won't be able to reach me for a while, but don't worry. I'm set to

go on a mission. Maybe I'll get the thrill back.
Bye."

Reese hung up the phone.

Chapter 2

It took a couple of weeks for her to settle into camp routine. Her spartan quarters were in a dormitory building with male and female instructor rooms on alternating floors. The recruits slept in barracks. Everyone ate in the mess hall where the food was decent. There was even a small private dining room where Barkley and his guests enjoyed table service.

She taught trainees how to use and maintain a variety of legal guns, including Berettas, SIGs and Glocks. With the extra time she'd had on her hands, she'd jogged and used the gym while staking out a number of locations in the camp. She'd even managed to shed a few pounds.

At first, Barkley and the other instructors kept their distance. She sensed she was being watched, but after her students placed at the top of all recruits tested for their automatic weapons knowledge and expertise, Barkley began to drop in on her classes, and sometimes stayed to talk about guns and fighting techniques. It was hard to conceal her animosity for the man, but she kept it under control. The other instructors gradually accepted her too.

Despite the number of racial minorities, a couple of white trainees made derogatory comments and racial slurs, but she'd put them in their place with some choice words and martial arts moves. She wasn't stupid, and knew too many fights would bring her unnecessary attention, so she'd shown restraint.

In what passed for a bar in the mess hall, Reese sat with a shot of tequila. Barkley's private dining room was closed. Other than exercise and training, there wasn't a lot to do. The mess hall opened for a couple of hours in the evenings so that the staff could relax with a drink or two. Sometimes, like tonight, there was even dancing.

Glancing around the room, she saw that the crowd was a mix of instructors, staff and a few recruits. The men and women at the facility were tough. Everyone was either a predator or a victim. Reese didn't intend to be a victim. With the reputation Flaherty had given her, someone would make her prove she'd earned her status, sooner or later. Reese was determined to pick her battles wisely.

The instructors had earned the right to keep their guns, but were also expected to use them with care. Therefore most of the fights involved fists, feet and knives, and usually served to establish whether you were a victim or a predator.

A solid figure settled on the seat next to hers. "Hey, sweet, want some bud?"

"No, and I ain't sweet." Reese sized him up and then went back to her drink. Of medium height with a stocky build, the man, Swanson, was somewhat attractive and sure of his welcome. She'd already seen enough to know the players in the training facility's drug supply trade. The slug who took a seat next to her was at the bottom of the food chain.

"If you say so, sugar. How about a dance?" he asked with a silly-looking leer.

"Look, I don't feel like dancing and I really don't feel like being bothered, so go away." A warning note crept into her voice.

"Come on ba-by." He leaned in close, his hand closing on her arm.

Reese went very still. Her eyes centered on where his hand gripped her arm. Then her voice cut through the noise in the room. "Get the hell out of my face!"

When he failed to release her, she stood, jerking out of his grip, her fists flying and landing on his nose and chin. The force knocked him out of his chair. Dazed for a moment, he looked up with blood running from his nose and a darkening bruise on his chin.

"Nobody puts their hands on me," she hissed.

His brows furrowed and his eyes shot sparks. "You don't know who you're messing with. I'm going to throw your ass through that front window. And then I might slice and dice that pretty face."

Widening her stance, she shot him a look of quiet menace. "Bring it on."

Wiping blood from his nose, he met her stare for a couple of beats. Something in her eyes made him falter. Then his right hand rose casually to touch the bulge of the gun in his jacket.

Reese's eyes narrowed. She wasn't going to let him pull a gun on her and get away with it. "Draw that gun you've got under your jacket and I swear you'll pull back a stump."

She lifted the shirt that covered the back of her camouflage print fatigues, where she kept the P226. "Feeling lucky?" Reese laughed, a low-down, dirty sound.

Swanson took a step backward and stopped. "This ain't over. I'll get you for this."

High on adrenaline, she faced the threat, ready to back up her words. "Fuck with me, and you won't be fucking anyone again, *ever*." Several people in the room laughed at that.

His face turned red, and he glared. Then he turned slowly and walked away.

Loud laughter and catcalls followed his exit.

Reese sat down and went back to her drink. She'd already seen the bartender press a button on the panel to summon backup.

As she sipped her drink, Barkley arrived with a couple of guards, guns drawn. That was quick. When they talked to the bartender, he shrugged and mumbled something. Barkley and the guards then turned to look at Reese. She pretended not to notice. Replacing their guns, the guards went to check outside.

The rush she'd felt during her fight with Swanson grew as she watched Barkley stop to chat with several people. She clenched her fist under the table. The dirty bastard. Just looking at his friendly, handsome face, you'd never guess the things he was capable of.

In an emotion-fueled fantasy she imagined herself drawing her SIG P226 pistol and shooting him where he stood, *for Riley.* Sweat broke out on her forehead as she savored the image, but kept one hand on her drink and the other under the table. *Remember the mission.*

Easing out a deep breath, she forced calm as he approached her, something akin to amusement glinting in his eyes.

"Having fun?" he asked, standing by her table, a dangerous aura lurking just beneath the surface.

"A little," she answered, the corners of her mouth turning up. "But he started it."

"And you finished it by kicking his ass. Or at least that's what I heard." Grinning back, controlled menace behind his green eyes, he shifted his feet. "Mind if I sit down?"

Forcing her back to relax into the chair, she tossed back the last of her tequila. "Help yourself."

Drawing a chair away from the table, he sat down and signaled the bartender for a round of drinks. "I enjoy seeing women in here, especially ones who can take care of themselves." He paused, his eyes alight with excitement, then continued. "I've got my eye on you, Whittaker. I'm picking folks for my steering committee and you're a prime candidate with the background, expertise and skills I want."

She was making progress. Inclining her head, Reese accepted another shot of tequila from the bartender and lifted it to thank Barkley. "Is this an invitation?"

The corners of his mouth lifted. "Let's call it a 'heads up.' I'm considering other candidates too."

Steadying herself, she tilted the shot glass to let the amber liquid burn a path down her throat. "Any other requirements?"

"Yeah, but I'd say you've got it covered." The look he gave her was not one that a manager or potential employer gave an applicant. He allowed a little heat to creep into his eyes.

Reese froze. She damn well wasn't going to sleep with Barkley to get on his committee and into his confidence. She racked her brain for a way to tell him without ruining her chances. "I'm ready and willing to do whatever's required of *all* the candidates," she said evenly.

Barkley laughed out loud, a wry, indulgent sound. "I wouldn't ask for anything else. One thing you're going to learn about me, Reese, is that I try to keep business and pleasure separate—and I'm usually successful."

"Then we have something in common," she said, directly meeting his gaze. The statement didn't reassure her. She suspected that somewhere down the line Barkley would hit on her. "What about money? I've always found that to be a good motivator."

He raised his brows. "If you make it onto the committee, your salary increases by a third and you'll have access to opportunities to make more."

"Sounds like something I'd like to do." She set her empty glass on the table.

Barkley drained his glass, his eyes measuring her. "Just hang in there. I'll be making my decision within the next couple of weeks. I don't remember when I've had so many good candidates to choose from. I only have room for a couple more people." He signaled for more drinks.

Reese gritted her teeth. She *had* to get on that committee. It would give her access to more locations to search for the code and help her find out about the illegal activities Barkley was involved in. "Who are the other candidates?" she asked, trying to glean more info.

Placing his elbows on the arms of his chair, he leaned forward slightly. "That I keep to myself to protect the candidates, but I've spoken to everyone. Someone has been terrorizing them with surprise attacks. One was seriously injured."

Reese's fingers curled restlessly beneath the table. She couldn't see why Barkley would tolerate someone preying on his candidates. Working the thought through, she reconsidered. Could Barkley know more about the perpetrator than he admitted? Maybe even used the situation as a test for the potential members of his committee?

"Who do you think is attacking them?" she asked, to see if she was right about her theory.

He shrugged, a hint of amusement in his eyes convincing her that he hadn't seriously looked into it.

"We don't know."

She had a hard time figuring Barkley out. He'd expressed concern, but she was picking up a different vibe. Was Barkley enjoying this? Was this all a game to him? "You think someone is trying to level the playing field?"

"Divide and conquer." Barkley's grin held boyish charm, but with an edge. He rubbed his jaw. "We *will* catch them, but until we do, it's an exciting time to be a candidate. Keep your guard up."

She would. Glancing around the room, she realized that the game had begun. Now that she was a candidate, she had to be ready to defend herself.

Staying alert for an anticipated attack twenty-four hours a day was difficult. As the days piled up, Reese did her best to stay on guard. It took a couple of weeks, but when she returned to her quarters after a late-evening run one night she sensed something in the dark as she reached for the light switch. In a violent rush of movement from behind the door, someone grabbed her by the sweatshirt and elbow and flung her into the wall. Stars exploded in her head. The door to her room slammed shut.

Stunned, she scrambled to her feet, finding her balance and searching for her attacker in the inky darkness. Hands seized her arm. She didn't wait to be thrown. Twisting, punching and kicking furiously, she managed to hold off her assailant. As they traded blows Reese realized that her opponent's skills matched hers. Strength of will fueled her resolve. She wasn't going to fail this test. With renewed energy, she fought with every down and dirty maneuver she'd ever learned, finally laying her opponent out cold.

Turning on the lights, she examined her attacker. Because she'd caught Drew Walters following her on more than one occasion, she'd half expected to see him instead of the red-haired stranger on the floor. That bothered her. She'd met all of the instructors—so where did this guy come from?

Reese called Barkley. Within minutes he arrived with guards and emergency techs. The emergency crew performed a quick check of Reese and her attacker, who was still unconscious. Reese noted that Barkley was the only one who recognized her attacker, and he didn't seem surprised.

When one of the emergency techs determined that the man on the floor had broken ribs and a possible concussion, Barkley shot Reese a look filled with admiration. "Good job. I figured that if any candidate would catch him, it would be you," he confided. "I'm impressed."

Angry that he'd play this game, she didn't respond. She could have been the one out cold on the floor, or worse.

Still pumped from the surprise attack, she suppressed a thread of guilt as they carried the red-haired attacker out on a stretcher. She'd done him good. She noticed that her knuckles were puffy from punching and blocking his blows.

As Barkley followed the crew out, he stopped and turned to Reese, his eyes narrowing. "Look, don't be so pissed about this. It's over and you won."

Startled that he could pick up on her emotions so easily, she nodded. "I'll get over it."

He grinned, his gaze turning calculating. "I wasn't wrong about you. With your background and everything you've demonstrated at this facility, you're just what we need on the steering committee. Congratulations."

Reese felt a load fall off her shoulders. She'd made it. Grinning, she shook Barkley's hand with her bruised one.

After he left, the excitement lasted through her hot shower and preparations for bed. Then she lay across the lumpy mattress with a splitting headache, cradling her bruised body. A couple of painkillers and a glass of water helped, but her thoughts drifted to Nick.

When she used to come home bruised from a mission, Nick would pamper her outrageously with a hot oil massage. After that, she usually fell asleep in his arms with an earful of endearments.

Reese flipped over to her side. *Nick is gone. You can't depend on him anymore.*

As soon as Reese discovered the location for the committee meetings, she met Larry on an evening run and they planted the small, bug-size pickup units in the tree outside the conference room and at strategic spots around the facility.

To cut down the risk of being caught, she didn't videotape the first two meetings she attended. Instead, she observed the other members and the way they interacted. Luckily, the only issues discussed involved the recruits. There were hints of new projects coming up.

In her quarters, Reese prepared for Barkley's committee meeting. She closed and secured the window. Then she sat at the desk and completed her check on the comm unit and the video camera. With the pickup unit outside the building, everything worked fine. Flaherty had confirmed it on the comm in her ear.

Leaving the dorm with bright sunlight tingling her skin, she crossed the sidewalk and walked three buildings over to the conference room. Outside the room, she reluctantly handed her SIG pistol, the knife she usually kept strapped to her thigh, and the stiletto she kept between her breasts to the attendant. She didn't worry about her earrings, which were too small to register on the metal detector.

Stepping through the archway of the security scan without incident, she entered the conference room—four white walls and one window—and stopped at the table in the back to make herself a cup of coffee. An old window air-conditioning unit whirred uselessly in a corner of the stuffy room.

Reese took a seat near the head of a hardwood table lined with Barkley's inner circle, a shady bunch of characters who'd already sold their souls to the devil. Eyeing the group calmly, she wasn't close to breaking a sweat. She realized that when it came to getting the job done, she wasn't much different from the steely-eyed characters seated in Barkley's conference room. Except, of course, that her job was helping to make the world safe from criminals like them.

Her eyes swept the handsome Arturo Bodega. He'd made a point of welcoming her to the group. Across from him in a blue jean jacket and pants sat Morrison, who kept to himself.

The thick envelope Flaherty had given her to study contained intelligence information on most of the people in the room. Reese had added a few observations of her own. Lana slipped into Barkley's quarters for horizontal recreation when she thought no one was looking. Walters had been having an affair with the private dining-room server. Reese noted that the poor woman had been bruised and beaten when she quit. It took Barkley a week to replace her.

Barkley entered the room and closed the door. The meeting began.

Her eyes felt dry and grainy. She'd spent half the night studying the bootleg copy of the camp's architectural plans that Larry had stolen from a contractor working on one of the camp's new buildings. The plans had narrowed the possibilities. Now all she and Larry had to do was check out each location and take advantage of any opportunities. Barring that, she'd find a way to make her own.

Shifting in her chair, she missed the feel of her SIG P226 pistol against the small of her back. Outside the room, instructors were allowed to keep their guns and knives as they had earned that right, but inside, Barkley insisted on a no-weapons policy for everyone but himself. He claimed that the policy had saved quite a few lives. Reese had her doubts. Most of the people in the room didn't need a gun or a knife to kill.

She let her fingers casually brush the leather sheath strapped to her thigh beneath the table. It usually held her knife beneath her favorite green camouflage fatigues. She liked the freedom that the roomy outfit, favored by the military and personally brought to camp, gave her.

Lifting her cup, she sipped coffee and listened to Barkley drone on.

"We've got that bunch of new recruits coming in next week. Now, I want their training done in half the regular six weeks' time. I've got some projects planned in the next month and a half that'll separate the wheat from the chaff."

"Sounds like a pay raise for anyone who survives." Stack chuckled, an eerie darkness in his eyes.

Barkley laughed at that, dimples forming in his cheeks. His good looks veiled a sharp mind and an agenda that had culminated in so many deaths. "An extra ten thousand to everyone who successfully completes my first new mission. Volunteers?"

Aware that Barkley's eyes were on her, Reese narrowed her own. "What's the mission?"

He flashed a smile full of charm, his eyes hardening. "You're either in or you're out. Need-to-know basis only, Reese, but from what I've seen of your skills, we could use you big-time."

Reese suspected that he was pulling together the team he would use to auction the satellite encryption codes on the international market. Because it was the first job to be brought to the committee since she'd joined, she didn't want to seem too eager or to volunteer for the wrong job. She set the cup down, her gaze cold.

"Let me think about it."

"What's there to think about?" he asked in a light tone. "We're talking seventy thousand, for planning and a day's work."

"I like the money," she said, meeting his gaze head-on.

"The pay is a lot more than time-and-a-half," Barkley urged, leaning forward.

"Are we doing a hit?" Walters asked, excitement evident in his voice. His beady black eyes were actually sparkling.

Stomach tightening, Reese worked hard to keep the disgust out of her facial expression. The dirty bastard liked to hurt women. She'd seen him eyeing her, especially since she'd had the run-in at the bar with Swanson.

"That's not the job, Walters," Barkley said coldly. "I don't waste my time with business like that."

"Why don't you just fill us in?" Lana asked, resting on her elbows so that several men at the table got a bird's eye view of her perfect breasts. Lana liked to tease. Barkley tossed her an impatient glance. Shrugging carelessly, Lana sat back. A collective sigh rose from some of the men.

"You all know the drill. Only the team going gets the details."

"Count me in." Rogers tossed a green poker chip into the center of the table.

"Count me in." Lana tossed her red chip in.

Holding on to her yellow chip, Reese chuckled inwardly at the irony. She was Susie Sunshine, all right.

Barkley held up one hand. "I'll name my dream team and they've got a day to decide. Then I'll ask for volunteers again." He looked around the table, weighing each person. "Whittaker, Walters, Bodega, Stack, Morrison and Rogers. Meeting's over."

"Humph!" Lana pushed her chair out.

Reese eased her chair back and pulled her five-foot-eleven-inch frame up slowly. Lana was watching her, still furious. Reese ignored her, knowing that the woman had more sense than to start something with her.

As she exited the room with the group, she picked up her gear. Outside, hot sun contrasted with a light, crisp breeze as she walked past the mission trails to a little park area. There, she climbed onto an old wooden picnic table and stood to look around. The green grass went on endlessly, and tall trees and bushes waved in the breeze. She hadn't been followed.

Reese sat down on the table and checked her watch. Five minutes early for her check-in. She spent the extra time watching for signs of being followed and forcing her thoughts away from her past. When she let her thoughts drift in that direction, weakness gripped her. She had to stay strong.

Barkley didn't allow cell phones and beepers at the camp. Guests and staff members were allowed to use the facility phones, but she knew that they were monitored. Thankfully, her comm unit was secure. She scanned the tree where the pickup unit was hidden. It never ceased to amaze her how this tiny piece of technology could take her signal, compress and encrypt it, and then beam it up to a communications satellite.

Massaging her ear to turn the link on, Reese spoke aloud. "Evan? Evan, are you there?" Then she waited, listening to the silence.

"Reese, I'm here." Flaherty's voice sounded in her ear with startling clarity. "How's it going?"

She spoke behind the cover of one hand, her gaze sweeping the grassy area and the line of trees the entire time. "Good. They trust me. I'll have the video cams going in the next meeting."

"Find anything?"

"No, but I've narrowed it down to the guarded

building on the other side of camp, the computer center, his office or his quarters. I'm concentrating on areas where there is tight security. I'll have to search his quarters alone, since Larry has no reason to be in the building, but I think Larry can neutralize the security system."

"When are you going to search it?"

"Tomorrow, when Barkley leaves for a meeting."

"We'll set you up for extraction. When you're ready, use the comm link. If there's a problem, just call the number we gave you and order pizza. After the call, you'll have an hour to get to the pickup point. Anything else?"

She hesitated. "Yeah. If it's not there, Barkley's bent on me being on a team for one of his special projects. I think he's getting ready to sell the code disk at the auction. If he is, I'll get a second chance at it."

"Be careful, Reese."

"I'm always careful," she said confidently.

Flaherty's voice softened. "I got a call from Nick this morning. He's recovered and has been fully debriefed. Reese—"

She gritted her teeth. She wished Flaherty would quit meddling. Sometimes he acted like her father, and that could be endearing, but not now. "Stay out of it, Evan. I'm focusing on this assignment. That's what you need me to do."

Evan sighed. "Yes, it is. Just be aware that since you're both still working for the agency, you might see him on a mission."

Reese swallowed hard, blinking against the sundrenched landscape that had taken on an air of surrealness. "I'll deal with it when it happens. Out."

"Out."

Massaging the area in front of her ear to turn off the comm, she caught movement out of the corner of her eye. Waiting, she saw a figure edging closer, using the cover of the trees to hide his approach. Pretending to look down at the table, she scanned the area.

Once she recognized the figure, adrenaline screamed through her veins. She knew that she would have to act. Stepping down from the table, she stood with her legs apart, ready to end this right now.

"Come on out, Walters," she called, squinting at the point where she'd seen him last. "I know you're there."

Chapter 3

Stepping out from behind a tree Walters began stalking across the grass-covered trail like the lethal predator he was. "Thought you might like a little company."

"I prefer my own company," Reese quipped. She noted the light sheen of sweat on his forehead. He seemed edgy. It didn't bode well for trying to talk him into leaving her alone.

He slowed his pace to pull out a knife and flick it open. "A stint in the Marines where you got yourself into a drugs and weapons cartel and now you come here and beat on Swanson in the bar.

You look like a woman, Reese, but you don't act like any woman I ever met. Today I'm going to find out just how much woman you are."

"Too much for you, Walters." Reese pulled her SIG from the back of her pants, locked and loaded and took aim. "Find another way to amuse yourself."

"Oh, but nothing compares to you, Reese," he replied, taking another step.

Looking down the sight, she squeezed the trigger. The bullet whizzed past the toe of his boots, taking a bit of the black leather with it.

With a loud curse, Walters leaped into the air. He threw her a furious glare. "You bitch!"

Again she took aim, interrupting him. "Take another step and I'll put a permanent part in your hair."

He let out a long, colorful string of curses.

She allowed the fresh breeze to buffer her, ready for his next move.

His gray eyes were feral, his fingers still clutching the knife. "You'd better make sure you kill me, because if you don't, I'm going to gut you like a fish."

"Then I'll take that under advisement and save a lot of time by putting a bullet through your brain," she said coolly. She heard the muffled sound of approaching footsteps on the grass. Too cautious to turn and look, she kept her distance and circled Walters until the newcomer was in her line of sight. It was Barkley. Reese focused on Walters, waiting to see what Barkley would do.

"What's going on here?" Barkley demanded.

Knife still in his hand, Walters glanced at him. "You heard her, boss. She's threatening to blow my brains out."

"That's what happens when someone pulls a knife on me and threatens to find out how much woman I am," she said in a measured tone.

Barkley eyed Walters with disgust. "I told you to stay away from the women!"

Walters let his gaze do a slow, heated perusal of Reese's curved but solid five-foot-eleven-inch frame. "I didn't think she counted. She's one of the boys in every other way."

"Don't be stupid!" Barkley snapped. "I need both of you in good shape for that job. If you want to kill each other, do it after the mission. If you need to let off steam, go ahead and kick each other's ass. I'm all for that." His tone lightened. "In fact, I'm looking forward to it."

Walters flicked his wrist and the knife disappeared.

Reese hesitated. Whatever it took, she had to

discourage Walters from ever stalking her again. Barkley seemed to know that. She stuffed the gun into the back of her pants. In a fluid movement she sprinted forward and used the momentum to snap out two solid front kicks, one to Walter's head and the other to his chest. She had the satisfaction of seeing his head snap back. Then he staggered.

Flipping over in the air in an acrobatic stunt she'd learned at the academy, she landed on her feet facing him with her arms and fists ready to block.

He grunted in pained surprise, raised his arms and turned his heavy frame to keep her in sight. Reese assessed his thick figure and the cold anger in his eyes. She'd have bet money that no other woman had ever had the guts to do what she'd done to Walters, and she wasn't finished yet. Raising her fists, she danced lightly on her feet, as if prepared to fight him the way another man would.

Walters advanced, letting her maneuver him so that the sunlight shone into his eyes.

Was she imagining the little smirk touching the corners of his thin lips? She guessed not, but she wasn't really stupid enough to move in close to go toe-to-toe with a man. Men in general had superior upper body strength to women. She could take a few punches and hold her own for a while, but if he was any good, she would be at a disadvantage. No, she had something more painful in mind for Walters.

Increasing her speed at the last moment, she feinted with her right, dodging his powerful left so that she only took a weakened blow from his right. His fist smashed into her and pain reverberated through her body. She caught her breath, staggering back a little, but managed to land a solid knee to his groin.

With a high-pitched cry, he doubled over in agony.

Intent on making sure he wouldn't forget this lesson, Reese caught his chin with a follow-up kick. Stunned, he hit the ground and lay there.

"That's enough!" Barkley shouted. "Whittaker, you've proven your point. Just look out when the mission is over, because I'll bet money he'll be after you."

Walters struggled to his feet, darkening bruises on his forehead and chin. "You bitch! I'm going to kill you!"

Standing her ground, she let him take two steps before she had the gun in her hand, her finger around the trigger. "One more step and I'll send you straight to hell—"

"One more step and if she doesn't kill you I will," Barkley snapped. "Now, Walters, pull your stupid ass together and pay attention. This woman isn't going to put up with your bullshit. Get back to your quarters!"

Dusting the grass from his pants, Walters turned and started back.

In the distance, Reese caught a distracting view of Bodega's buff, bronzed body in shorts and T-shirt, as he jogged one of the trails. To his left, Larry walked around the camp trail in a baggy shirt and pants. She knew that Larry's outfit hid his sniper gun and that he had been covering her back while she checked in, but what was Bodega up to?

Barkley eyed her carefully. "Reese Whittaker, you are one hell of a woman! You all right?"

Reese nodded, slowly rotating her shoulder on the side where Walters had hit her. It hurt even though she was still pumped from the fight. She'd be lucky if she could move the shoulder in the morning. "I'm fine."

"I think you might seriously want to volunteer for my little project about now," Barkley prompted.

Reese nodded. He was right. It was time to throw in on his project. "I volunteer," she said pleasantly.

"Good! I could use your expertise." He turned and strolled back to the main buildings with her. "By the way, nice show back there."

Still giddy from the rush, Reese laughed and thought how she'd like to "show" Barkley just how good she would be at kicking his ass.

Dinner in the mess hall reminded Reese of the family-style steak houses where her grandmother used to treat her and Riley with the long, dark wooden tables, except that the crowd included no families and there was only a low buzz of conversation. A few diners sat together, talking about the day's activities. Most sat alone, too hard-core and suspicious to be friendly with anyone.

After quickly finishing her meal and then scanning the hall and the adjoining private dining room, Reese slipped into the kitchen with her plate for a quick word with Larry. The kitchen fans provided a comfortable level of noise and the cook was busy at the grill with several steaks. An assistant made bread in a separate area, and Larry worked with vegetables and salads.

"The search list," she murmured, stuffing the

paper into his apron and using her body to shield the transfer. "Meet me in the upper hall at twelve tonight and we'll check out the first prospect."

"You volunteered for his assignment," Larry whispered incredulously before she could walk away.

"Didn't have much choice," she shot back. "I think it's the auction for the disk."

"You don't want to go on this mission," Larry warned. "It isn't about the disk. I think it's got something to do with a biological weapon. I've seen the lab equipment he's buying for it."

"Then I'm still in. I can't take the chance on him endangering more people. Besides, if we get what we came for tonight, Barkley will be in prison and there won't be another mission," she said.

"And if we don't?"

"We will." Reese sensed movement behind her. She'd been watching the kitchen doorway. "Are you sure you don't have some turnip greens in there somewhere?" she asked.

"Today's vegetable is steamed spinach with bacon and onions," Larry explained, lifting the top off a large pot. "Want some?"

She shrugged, wrinkling her nose but considering it. She'd never had spinach with bacon and onions. "I guess."

Shifting on her feet, she glanced behind her. Barkley stood there, a curious expression on his face.

"Finding everything you need?" Barkley asked.

"Everything but turnip greens." She accepted the bowl from Larry and stuck her plate in a pan of dirty dishes.

Barkley faced Larry. "Make sure you have turnip greens for Ms. Whittaker tomorrow."

"Yes, sir." Larry went back to his salads.

"Join me in the private dining room," Barkley directed, leading the way. "You should use the private dining room and let Michelle get what you need."

Reese said nothing. At the last staff meeting, Barkley had informed them that they could eat in the private dining room if there were no guests. Because she hated waiting to be served, she'd continued to eat in the regular mess hall. Before easing into the kitchen, she'd noted that the private dining room had several people waiting for service.

Now, as the kitchen door closed, Reese glanced at the swamped server, then pointedly back to Barkley.

"You have a point," he conceded. "We could

use another server." He followed her to a table and sat down.

What was his game? she wondered. According to rumor, she wasn't his type, but he'd certainly been in her face enough during the past two or three weeks to make her wonder. This contrasted with the fact that he was still getting his rocks off with the petite, blond-haired, blue-eyed Lana.

Reese sat so that their legs would not touch. It was hard enough to treat the man normally knowing that he was responsible for her brother's death. Making small talk was almost asking too much. Glancing away, Reese reminded herself that she could do anything, even make small talk with a prick like Barkley, if it would bring him to justice.

Barkley motioned the server over, got water and ordered a bottle of Jack Daniel's. Reese drank water and tried the spinach.

Sipping whiskey, he leaned closer and said, "I'm glad you decided to volunteer for my little project."

"Really?" She pasted on a half smile, hoping the whiskey would loosen his tongue. "You never got around to telling me what you had in mind."

"Once you're all briefed on the mission, I'll

want your advice on the weapons to get the job done, the best way to execute the project, and input on keeping everybody safe. I've already got you down for a key role."

"Sounds like it might be real exciting," she prompted, finishing the bowl of tasty spinach.

At his request, the waitress brought another glass. Filling it with Jack Daniel's, Barkley nudged it toward Reese. Thanking him, she urged him to continue.

"It *will* be exciting," he said, anticipation lighting his eyes. "And dangerous." Filling his glass again, he continued. "This mission is big. If things go the way I plan, I may never have to work again."

Reese lifted an eyebrow. "And no one else is going after this?"

Barkley let a self-satisfied smile settle on his face. "It's not the sort of thing that people publicize, and I'm keeping close tabs on my source to make sure this doesn't get out."

"So who are you lining up to pay for it? The government? Foreign governments? Terrorist organizations?"

Barkley shrugged. "I'm an equal opportunity businessman, but I've already got a prospective buyer. If someone wants to beat that offer, I'm open. If they don't, who cares?"

I do. I'm not going to let you help someone hurt my country. She grinned and said, "I'm looking forward to our meeting tomorrow."

In her room at last, Reese set her clock for eleven-thirty because she slept harder when she drank alcohol, especially whiskey.

Her body throbbed and ached from her fight with Walters. In the shower, she let the massage spray hit the bruised areas of her chest and shoulder for several minutes.

When she finally stretched out on the bed to sleep, her mind was racing. She went over the plans for her and Larry's search of the guarded building on the other side of the camp tonight. Tomorrow she would try Barkley's quarters.

Her mind focused in on the odd light she'd seen in Walters's eyes when he threatened her earlier today. She'd taught him a lesson, yeah, but would it keep him from coming after her? Somehow she doubted it. She liked to stay at least two steps ahead of her opponents. She got up and double-checked the door. Then she placed a chair beneath it. If Walters made it through that, she'd be waiting for him.

Turning over, she punched the pillow and lay on the bed, breathing in and out deeply. As sleep drifted over her, she relaxed and stretched out her hand...to touch Nick....

Jerking back, Reese was suddenly wide awake as she sat up in the bed, reaching for cigarettes that weren't there. The lawyer had probably served Nick with the divorce papers already. If she had been around, he'd be busy trying to talk her out of it. She wasn't that weak.

Now she would be a free woman. Now Nick would be free to stay at the agency and do what he loved best, while she moved on to her own bigger and better things.

She eased back down on the bed. She'd been through the wringer with the agency shrink about what she'd been doing with Nick. The shrink's portion of the requalification sessions had only confirmed it. She'd been trying to construct that perfect, loving little family unit that neither she nor Nick had ever had.

Dedicated to their country and careers, her parents' marriage had been a cordial arrangement. Often away on assignment, they loved Reese and Riley, but were always happy to return to work.

Nick's mother abandoned him when he was eight, so he grew up in foster care, where he was sometimes abused and mistreated. Belonging was important to him, because of the love and security he'd missed growing up. Before she'd come along, the Agency had been Nick's family. Maybe it would never change.

Nick was good, yeah. He'd been the best, with the physical assets and personal integrity she admired. She'd never clicked with any man so well or stayed around long enough to reach the depth of emotion he inspired. Smooth, smart and extremely competent, he'd shown her warmth and real love. *Better to have loved and lost...*

At eleven-thirty sharp, her eyes opened in the darkness. Dressing quickly, she donned a black shirt and pants, taking care to stow her SIG pistol in the small of her back and her 9 mm spare in her boot. Adjusting her bra, she added the stiletto, a small grenade, and her night-vision goggles into her belt pouch. Then she covered her hair with a balaclava.

As she stepped into the hall and closed the door, her mind replayed some of Walters's threats. Had he really given up? The male instructors and staff members had rooms on the next floor. She peered into the darkness, ready for anything. When nothing happened, she made her way down the hall. Treading carefully, and timing her exit so that the rotating infrared camera failed to document it, she hit the stairs at a light run.

At the lower level, Larry stepped out of one of the dark doorways. "From what I could gather when I scouted earlier, where we're going isn't under electronic surveillance. If it is, it's on a different system," Larry whispered.

"We'll just have to be careful and play it by ear," she whispered back, leading the way to the back door.

With the exception of the lighted pathways and the security lights of several buildings, the camp was quiet and dark. Security guards backed up with surveillance cameras worked the gates and patrolled the camp at somewhat predictable intervals.

Reese and Larry watched the guards make their rounds from the safety of the shrubs. Then, under the cover of darkness, they made their way to the guarded building, known as Building 22.

Where two guards usually stood, a lone security guard paced with a rifle slung across his shoulder. At Reese's signal, Larry pulled out a device he'd programmed to disrupt electricity in the building and began to play with the buttons.

The guard looked up as the lights started to flicker. Reese and Larry heard him cursing loudly as the lights went out. They sprinted noiselessly into the building and then to the basement as the guard went for the circuit-breaker panel on the first floor.

Reese slipped down the corridor checking for cameras and security apparatus.

She was heading back to Larry a few minutes later when she heard footsteps echoing in the corridor from the other end. Her heart slammed into her chest. Fingers fumbling with the pouch at her waist, she melted into the dark doorway of one of the closed rooms. She peered around the doorway, drawing the 9 mm, the silencer already in place. It was another security guard, his flashlight beam knifing through the darkness at her end of the hall. The guard was walking toward her. She didn't want to kill the guard, but if he found her and Larry in the building, she'd have no choice. Dead men told no tales.

The footsteps got louder as he neared. Sweat trickling down her brow, she raised the gun, her fingers closing on the trigger.

The guard dropped his flashlight in a sudden clamor of noise. As he scrambled to retrieve it, Reese used the commotion to leave the doorway. Then, from across the hallway, she watched him swing the arc of his flashlight at the remaining doors before turning to go back up the stairs.

Stepping out of the shadows, Reese opened the door to what appeared to be a maintenance closet. Larry was inside the cramped space which contained a large sink, a couple of mops and a bucket.

"All clear?" he asked, his gun still drawn. He got an "A" for not shooting her.

"It's clear," she assured him. "We'd better get on with it. The other security team will be back in about an hour."

Turning around, Reese moved on to the next door, shining her light through the window. The room was empty.

Guns drawn, they went back up the corridor. They paused at a locked room with fancy, double-glass doors reinforced with steel. There was no sound coming from the room. Stepping forward, Reese made short work of the lock, noting that the electronic part of it had not yet been connected. She turned the handle and pushed the door open.

Barkley was apparently turning the area into some sort of lab. It consisted of two rooms, the inner room constructed almost entirely of double-paned safety glass. Equipment and boxes were everywhere. Reese recognized a mass spectrometer next to the expensive refrigeration system. A high-end climate-control system had already been installed. Several boxes of High Efficiency Particulate Air filters—HEPA filters—littered the floor, some empty. An electronic surveillance system that had yet to be installed sat next to the wall. What was Barkley up to?

On the other side of the room, Larry was checking boxes. "Get a load of this!"

Anticipation peaking, she hurried over. He'd opened one of the large, brown boxes in the middle of the floor and was bent over the contents. An orange and black synthetic suit of some kind was in the box. Larry drew out the headpiece. A clear, plastic area fit over the face, with a circular plastic connector over the nose and mouth area.

"This is for the filter and air supply," Larry told her.

"It's a biohazard suit," she said, removing a pair of heavy, black plastic gloves. "It's similar to the suits people wear when they're making drugs."

"Yep. Remember I told you that Barkley was up to something involving bio-weapons?"

She stuffed the gloves back into the box.

"Yeah, and I don't like it. Let's check out the rest and get back to our quarters."

Though rushing, they were careful to put the boxes and equipment back the way they'd found them. Then they explored the rest of the area. She was shocked to find two soundproof and airtight rooms on the corridor held men, obviously prisoners.

Reese peered into the one-way glass on the magnified sight hole on each steel-reinforced door to see beds, a bathroom corner, and a table for eating or reading in each room. Both men wore blue hospital scrubs. Neither Reese nor Larry recognized the men, but they regretted the fact that they could not free them. Not yet. Besides, the men could very well have been quarantined due to illness. She suspected that they were guinea pigs for one of Barkley's projects. The rest of the rooms were either empty or being used for storage.

Reese checked her watch. "We've got fifteen minutes."

Separating, they retraced their steps to make sure everything was left the way they'd found it.

Minutes later she met Larry out front and they melted into the bushes and sprinted down a trail. Keeping low, they made it to the shed in the wooded area near the shooting range. Reese

called Flaherty on her comm unit and filled him
in quickly.

"I want you to go on Barkley's mission," Flaherty said.

Not surprised, Reese argued anyway. "What
about the codes? What are we going to do about
them? Aren't we losing focus here?"

"No, we're not losing focus," Flaherty said,
strongly emphasizing each word. "If Barkley's
planning something with bio-weapons, then the
danger is more immediate. The lives of millions
of people could be at stake. Retrieving the decipher code is still important. Larry can look for it
while you and Barkley are gone."

Reese slowly let out the breath she'd been
holding. "Okay, I'm on it."

"Do they screen for electronic devices before
they let you into Barkley's conference room?"
Flaherty asked.

"Yes. You walk through a system that identi-
fies guns, explosives and electronic devices. I've
gotten the earrings through by keeping them
turned off. The comm unit is also turned off and
so small that it is virtually undetectable."

"I know there's a risk involved, but I want you
to have your comm on in the meeting, so we can
listen in."

"Will do, Chief. It'll be off until I've made it into the conference room. Anything else?"

"Yeah." Flaherty's voice softened. "Be careful out there. Larry, too."

As soon as they ended the phone conversation, Reese looked at Larry. "Have you got a plan?" she asked, giving him an opportunity to ask for help.

"Yeah." Larry shifted against the wall in the shed, trying to look confident. His voice sounded a little strained. "I'll get all the intel on Barkley's quarters, and as soon as you guys take off, search them for the disk."

"That should work," she told him. "Any problems at all, call Flaherty. He can extract you or send backup. Do you remember the extraction plan?"

"Oh, yeah," Larry swallowed. "That's my life-line."

"It really is." Reese clapped him on the shoulder, searching for something comforting to say and coming up short. She couldn't help looking at him and wondering if he was going to make it. He'd had her back when Walters came after her and he'd been good on the sweep they'd made on Building 22, but she still lacked a feel for how he would do on his own.

Larry was watching her with a curious expression on his face. She realized that the time for saying something encouraging had passed. Shaking his hand, she said, "See you around, Larry. Good luck."

"Yeah, you too."

Silent now, they left the shed to fade into the darkness and head back to their quarters, intent on the new turn of events. Things were now a lot more dangerous. If what they suspected was true, the price on Barkley's head had just gone up.

Chapter 4

Reese arrived at the conference room ten minutes early. She was anxious to hear Barkley's briefing and determined to get through the security check without witnesses that might inspire the guard and attendant to be more thorough.

She drew her SIG pistol, knife, and the 9 mm backup and gave them to the big, beefy attendant. Used to the routine, he passed her through without checking her further. With all the confidence in the world, she stepped through the scanning machine.

The attendant stopped chatting with the guard

to stare at his screen. "You're clear, Ms. Whittaker," he said respectfully, his gray eyes centered on her breasts.

After inclining her head in acknowledgment, she walked into the conference room.

At the table along the wall at the back of the room, Bodega was pouring himself a cup of coffee. "Coffee?" he asked in his sexy accent.

A warm glow started around her middle and spread right through her. "Sure," she answered in as professional a voice as she could muster. Placing her notebook on the table, she walked the length of the conference table to join him.

"You didn't seem too inclined to join the team yesterday, but I'm glad you did," he said in a conversational tone. "Cream and sugar?"

His voice sent small ripples of heat to her center. He might as well have offered himself, too.

"Yes," she answered. She focused on his coffee, noting that he drank it black. Most of the instructors did. She'd tried, but had never gotten the hang of it. It probably cost her a few "cool" points, but she didn't care.

Reese watched Bodega's bronze fingers pour the cream into her cup and stir the mixture with one of the thin, wooden stirrers.

"I wasn't sure I wanted to volunteer for this

mission, but after Walters and I got into it yesterday, it seemed like the thing to do." Accepting the cup from Bodega, she thanked him.

"I was out running, so I saw some of your altercation," he said, long black lashes dropping down and then rising over eyes the rich brown color of good cognac. "You handled yourself well."

"Thank you." She couldn't keep the smile from spreading across her face. Bodega was one of the best that the facility had to offer in hand-to-hand combat, so his compliment meant a lot. Then there was the matter of the potent male charm he radiated. She couldn't stop her pulse from speeding up a little. Bodega was eye candy of the highest caliber. She could feel the pure masculine magnetism drawing her in.

Bodega was the type of man to flirt and have fun with. Hell, she would have bet a couple of hundred that he was good in bed. However, he was not the kind of man a woman wanted for keeps. *You thought the same thing when you met Nick,* she reminded herself as she took a sip of her coffee. That was a sobering thought. Was that where she'd gone wrong? She should have listened to her gut instinct about Nick.

"So? Did I do a good job?" he asked, leaning closer.

He'd done a good job of getting her motor started. Staring straight into his eyes, she had the feeling that he had an idea of the direction that her thoughts had taken. "Excuse me?"

He grinned. "The coffee. Is that how you like it?"

"Yes. It's perfect." Reese bit the inside of her lip as their gazes locked.

The background noise of other people entering the room broke their connection. Someone came up to get a cup of coffee. She thanked Bodega and left to take her seat at the table with the others. Luckily, she'd strategically placed her notebook on the table in front of an available seat near the window for the least interference for her comm.

Brushing her hair off her face, she casually adjusted her earrings, turning the cameras on. Resting her face on her knuckles, she used a forefinger to massage the area just in front of her ear.

Flaherty's voice sounded in her ear. "Reese, the comm and the camera are up and running. If you can hear me, touch your right earring."

Resting her face in her hand, she let a finger touch the earring. Then she relaxed. She'd been holding herself in, to keep from reacting when Flaherty came on line.

In fatigues identical to those she wore, Barkley entered with an older, white-haired man she'd never seen before. He did not exude testosterone like most of the occupants of the room. His gray suit hung on him like a weighted sack as he gazed nervously around.

Motioning his guest to a seat, Barkley sat at the head of the table. "I want to thank all of you for volunteering for my little project. It's going to make all of us a lot of money. Let's get started."

He took his remote and switched on the media screen mounted on the wall alongside the table. When he clicked the remote again, the screen displayed a large laboratory complex in a land-scaped, rural area. "This is the Harwell Middle-house Biotechnology Laboratory in Waikeeno Falls, New Jersey. They do a lot of work creating drugs to combat viruses. They also develop vaccines. In the past, they've had contracts with the government to find antidotes and cures for ill-nesses encountered by our troops during war."

Barkley paused to pour himself a glass of water from the plastic pitcher on the table. The sound of the water filling the glass followed by Barkley swallowing were the only noises in the room. Enjoying the attention, he set the glass down and resumed his briefing.

"Several months ago, a company scientist was in Africa working with the World Health Organization. A number of workers at the hospital where he was stationed came down with a new, unidentified virus that infected and killed eighty percent of the staff. As one of the lucky, uninfected survivors, he brought back samples of the virus with the hope of developing a cure. In a lab accident several months ago, the virus killed all who came in contact with it. Luckily, the scientist who brought it back was not on site at the time. He has since been kidnapped and the virus taken by the terrorist group Viper. The scientist has been forced to work on the cure for what is being called the African Rage virus."

With the comm fitted inside her ear, Reese was the only one who heard Flaherty cursing under his breath and ordering Rage virus intelligence information. The comm abruptly went silent.

Reese sat at the table with her face carefully blank. A virus. She could guess where Barkley was going with this and she didn't like it. He wasn't content to go after any of the established bioweapons. No, he was going after something new and lethal. There were millions of lives at stake. Straightening her shoulders, she thought of the many times she'd managed to beat the odds in the past. She could do it again, whatever it took to stop Barkley.

The group stared at Barkley, anticipating his next words. He settled into his seat at the table, leaving the media screen on. "If you're all wondering what this has to do with you, *we* are going to get that virus and bring it back to the lab I'm building on this facility. We'll also bring back Dr. Marshall Ballinger, the scientist working on the cure, so he can continue his work here."

Reese clutched the edges of her chair beneath the table. Damn, she hated being right.

Barkley motioned to his guest. "This is Dr. Phil Reynolds, who worked with Ballinger at Harwell Middlehouse. He'll train us to safely transport and store the virus, and brief us on the virus and work done on the cure before it was stolen."

Barkley pressed a button and several buildings and complexes flashed across the screen; some modern and others old and rundown. "Viper likes to hide behind legitimate businesses. We think they're backing a pharmaceutical company, Lorenza, with labs in South and Central America. We've got our hands on the architectural details for several of their labs and we're working to pinpoint the exact location of Ballinger and the virus.

Meanwhile, we have pictures of the insides of several of the complexes, and you'll all get copies of the building plans, electrical systems, alarms, and everything else we could find to put together our plan."

Pausing for a moment, he glanced around the table once more. "Before we get to your questions and the next briefing, let's discuss roles on my team. As always, I will lead this project. And this room is full of supremely talented individuals." His gaze singled Reese out. "Whittaker, you'll act as point man and my backup lead. Bodega, you're my second, and backup for Reese. Walters, Morrison, you're security. Rogers, you'll work team decontamination and virus-handling with Dr. Reynolds. Mick and Carlos are already in-country, watching the labs and gathering information. Any comments or complaints?"

Reese found Walters staring at her hard. His beady black eyes bulged, his jaw tightened. She guessed that he was still furious about their fight, and wondered if he'd be stupid enough to bring up the problem he had with her. Barkley was just as likely to fix the problem with the 38-caliber pistol he kept under his jacket.

Barkley leveled a menacing stare at each individual in the room. "I'm going to say this once, and next time I'll simply deal with troublemakers as I see fit. For the duration of this project, we are a special team. Any issues or problems you have with one another are suspended until this is over. Is that clear?"

Everyone nodded in agreement. It took several seconds, but Walters's angry facial expression finally smoothed into one that displayed little emotion. Barkley opened the floor for questions to himself and Reynolds.

Bodega spoke first. "Dr. Reynolds, what is your background and training?"

Pale blue eyes stood out in a tan but lined face as Reynolds gave his background in a cultured voice. "I am a medical doctor with degrees from Johns Hopkins University. I am also a researcher with specialized training and experience in the areas of virology and bacteriology from several universities and government projects. I've been at Harwell Middlehouse Biotech for five years and personally worked on the project dealing with Gulf War illnesses. I have experience with the Rage virus too."

"Do we have the proper equipment and setup for handling the viruses?" Reese asked, thinking of the area she'd investigated with Larry.

Reynolds hesitated, his gaze quickly flitting

around the room to settle on Barkley. Reese saw Barkley give an almost undetectable nod before the man continued.

"Not at present, but I have been working with Mr. Barkley and his staff to ensure that we have our Biosafety Level 4 facility ready for our project. This will be designed to prevent infectious microbes from being released into the environment and provide the highest possible level of safety for everyone working with the viruses. The specific measures we will be employing include micro-filtration of air, air-lock buffer zones, 'space suits' with positive-pressure air supply, chemical decontamination, and decontamination at high temperature for long periods of all materials used in the facility."

Flaherty talked to Reese over the comm. "Reynolds had a nervous breakdown after the accident at the lab. He's still unstable. They haven't released him for work yet. We're still checking Department of Defense, Department of Health, and FBI records and contacts, but it looks as if the biotech company failed to report all of the pertinent facts to the government. The company has been fined for their virus-handling techniques, but there is nothing in the files specifically naming the African Rage virus except for some records of a deadly virus that killed a lot of people in a remote area in Africa."

Reese finished her coffee. She'd been wondering how a man like Reynolds could join with a man like Barkley and try to exploit something that had such grave consequences. Now she had an answer. Reynolds was a nutcase.

"What are the symptoms of the virus?" Reese asked. "And how long does a person live once they've been infected?"

Reynolds's silence went on for so long that she became convinced he wasn't going to answer. His voice was raspy as old sandpaper when he began, the words falling on the group like a death sentence.

"Symptoms include high fever, confusion, muscle pain and severe headache. Within a couple of days, it progresses to vomiting, diarrhea, abdominal pain, sore throat, rash and chest pain. This disease attacks internal organs and the ability of blood to clot. To be specific, the organs in the body liquefy. All victims have died within three to four days."

Reese's throat went dry and her stomach tightened. This virus was some serious shit. The team would need to be on alert at all times to avoid getting infected.

Staring into Reynolds's tired blue eyes, she saw a man still haunted by the part he must have played in the loss of human lives, but furious over his company's attempt to eliminate him from the project. Perhaps that fury had fueled his deal with Barkley.

By the time the team broke for lunch, Reese was feeling the strain from her mind racing a thousand miles ahead. How was she going to make sure that the new virus was either destroyed or given to government scientists for study and development of a cure? She'd have to seize every opportunity.

Barkley insisted on them all eating lunch together in a new, separate dining room that was just big enough for the team. Reese felt like a prisoner. It was a good thing she'd worn her comm. Flaherty had heard everything and she'd made certain that the video cameras in her earrings captured all the maps, plans and briefing materials.

"Now that we're an official project team, we'll spend most of the remaining time together. There will be no communication with people outside the group. You will each be escorted back to your room to gather enough of your personal items to last a few weeks," Barkley told them over lunch.

"By then we should have completed the project and our first sale."

"You have a buyer already?" Walters asked, his bug eyes gleaming.

"Oh, yes," Barkley told him in a voice teeming with excitement. "And the price goes up if our scientist friend finds a cure."

She met Barkley's penetrating stare with an approving nod every now and then to show her support, but anger and outrage vibrated so strongly inside her that she didn't dare speak.

She'd been planted in the camp for a purpose and it was proving to be a hell of a lot more important than the satellite software encryption codes and revenge on Barkley. What she'd heard sickened her. Thousands of people might die a horrible death so that Barkley could pad his pockets.

With the hour of free time they were given after lunch, Reese gathered her clothing, toiletries, a few books, and the lipstick gun and sharp-edged polymer knife that she'd been given at CIA headquarters. The entire time she packed, one of the guards watched from the doorway to ensure that she communicated with no one aside from the team members.

Flaherty's voice filled her comm with his

thoughts on what he'd seen and heard in her meeting. He was planning to use the information she'd gathered to send a CIA team in to scoop up the virus before Barkley did. That made Reese part of the backup team—and she didn't like it.

Reese hadn't worked backup in years. Unfortunately, there was little she could say to Flaherty with a guard watching her every move and listening to the noises she made in response to Flaherty's questions.

When she'd finished packing, she followed the guard to her new room in a building in a restricted area on the other side of the camp.

Her new quarters were spacious and located at the end of a hall, next to an exit door. If she tried hard, she could almost believe that she was in a hotel. A soft but firm, comfortable bed and a large, blue modular desk complete with a computer and printer were the largest pieces of furniture in the room. There was even an oversize picture window with a garden view, television, DVD player, coffeemaker and alarm clock. The only negatives were the fact that Barkley's quarters were right across the hall and Walters's were two doors down.

She ignored the little rush of pleasure she got at the thought that Bodega's quarters were right next door.

* * *

Beneath a wall sporting a framed color photograph of a ten-year-old Riley and a twelve-year-old Reese behind a birthday cake, Nick Whittaker hugged his sister-in-law, Carol, and said all the comforting things people say when loved ones die. He knew that wherever Reese was, she was devastated too. The bond between Reese and her brother had been so strong that he'd sometimes felt left out.

The agency had finally allowed him to go home. The weakness still lingering in his body made him tire easily. He hadn't fully recovered from the dysentery and parasites he'd picked up in South America.

Feeling a little too warm in the cheerful living room, he loosened his tie and slipped a couple of buttons on his starched shirt. As he eased back onto the couch, his gaze fell on a photo of his father-in-law, Chief Warrant Officer Kelly Blackstone.

He'd seen the old man at Riley's memorial site, looking like a lost soul. At one point the old man had simply looked at him and said, "She left you, huh?"

Speechless and shaken, Nick hadn't answered. He couldn't. Eventually, Blackstone had moved away to spend a few silent moments at the memorial that had been erected for his son.

Nick still didn't know where Reese was, and the agency wasn't talking. He missed his wife with a bone-deep ache that was constant.

He'd come back to the house with Carol to offer some comfort, but he'd also hoped to glean something about Reese's mission, or at least find out how long she might be gone. He should have known better. Reese was a competent professional in every sense of the word. She'd left no clues.

He lifted Riley's angel, Candy, for one last baby kiss on the cheek. That was the hardest part. Would his daughter have grown to look as sweet and precious as Candy? The thought constricted his chest.

Reese had to understand. He'd made a choice to rescue innocent people because he was the only available agent with an intimate knowledge of the Colombian countryside and the rebels involved. He hadn't chosen to abandon her, to leave her to go through the loss of their child alone.

Being served with divorce papers at their home had been the last straw. That Reese wanted to be free of him and had taken it this far reinforced the fact that he had lost everything that mattered in his life. It had taken every bit of control that remained to keep himself from taking out his pain and frustration on the guy who served the papers.

The puffed silk of Candy's bangs brushed his cheek and one fat braid rested against his neck. "Don't go, Uncle Nick," she begged in a soft, high-pitched voice.

"Honey, I have to, but I'll be back."

Big golden brown eyes just like Reese's beseeched him. "Please, Uncle Nick." Her arms locked around his neck.

Nick stilled, his eyes searching her face and hating the sadness he saw there. He held her closer and rocked her back and forth until she fell asleep.

After carrying the sleeping child to her room and placing her in bed, he took off her shoes and covered her with the bedspread. He stood for a moment at the door to watch her sleeping peacefully, then turned off the light.

In the living room, Carol was pacing the floor. Eyes bright with tears stood out in a face gone thin and gaunt from loss of weight. She obviously wasn't eating. He took her in his arms and said a silent prayer for their family.

In the morning, he'd report back to the agency. Ironically, it might be the only way to get Reese back.

Chapter 5

Reese sat in the new conference room on the other side of the compound. They were ordered to limit their interaction with the other camp guests.

Barkley was briefing the team on the computer models of the two Viper labs that he considered the most likely targets. He took them on a virtual tour, pointing out to the team each possible point of entry to the labs, where the guards were usually stationed, and where the cameras were. Everyone studied the screen.

"We'll break for today, and tomorrow we'll

get into the alarm systems," Barkley said, his eyes bright with barely contained excitement. "The plan is almost ready for execution."

The group broke up, some people heading for the dining area, others going out for a smoke, and still others heading to their rooms for a quick nap. Reese was one of the latter. She wasn't hungry and hadn't been sleeping well since Barkley had disclosed their mission. The need for sleep was so powerful that she was actually dreaming of her nice, soft, comfortable bed. It was calling to her. As she headed for her room, however, Bodega followed her.

"You're tired," he said.

"Yeah." Reese yawned. "I guess the excitement of the mission has been keeping me up."

"So you're going to bed now?" he asked as they entered the building that housed their new rooms.

"I don't have much choice," she answered. They traveled down the hall toward her room. "I don't think I could stay awake long enough to eat dinner."

Bodega's voice took on a provocative tone as they reached her door. "That's too bad, because I was hoping we could enjoy each other's company."

That got her attention. She looked up to find his gaze hot and enticing. It was hard to keep her eyes off the bronze muscular chest with the sprinkling of dark hair revealed by the two unfastened buttons at the top of his white cotton shirt. She already knew he had a hot body after seeing him run in just a tank top and shorts. So she wasn't too tired to appreciate his charms after all.

"I *am* enjoying your company."

"Then perhaps you'll let me come inside?" His gaze bore holes through the front of her fatigues. What he wanted was obvious.

Staring into those dark, sexy eyes, Reese smiled at the double entendre. Was she going to let Bodega inside? If she did, it would be a turning point for her, an affirmation that she really was over Nick.

"Please?"

She liked it when men said *please.* "For a little while." The words tumbled out without permission from her brain.

Deciding to see where this would take her, she checked to make sure no one was watching them, then turned and fit her key into the lock. What was she doing? She didn't have an answer.

Unlocking the door, she pushed it open. Bodega stepped through boldly, then waited for her to close the door. She did, and leaned back against it, waiting to see what he would do.

He moved in close to cup her face in his hands. "I've been thinking about you," he whispered. "Day and night." With a fingertip, he touched her eyelid and trailed his fingers down to her lips. "Your eyes, your lips…"

She felt the heat of his hands, warm against her skin, curving along the fullness of her breasts and sliding down to outline the swell of her hips.

"Your breasts, your hips… Perhaps I'm dreaming. Reese, you are a goddess. Are you real?"

She wanted him, wanted to kiss those lush lips that graced his face full of angular planes, thrust her fingers into his thick, curling hair, and feel that strong, muscular body on hers. Reese's body throbbed with anticipation, but she held back, waiting for him to make his move.

"Why don't you find out?" she challenged.

"I thought you'd never ask." His mouth covered hers hungrily, nibbling and sucking at her lips.

A mounting wave of desire gripped her. She gasped, and, sliding her hands against the warm skin of his chest, she met his tongue with her own, curving, thrusting and sliding in a dance that mimicked what her body longed to do.

His fingers massaged her nape, moving down past her shoulders to skim her waist and grip her buttocks. Hot and hard, he rotated himself against her.

Reese groaned at the pleasurable sensations bombarding her body.

"Say yes," he demanded in a whisper as he backed her toward the bed.

"Yes," she obliged, drawing the word on a long, heartfelt sigh. "Do you have protection?" She fell back on the bed, her head sinking into the fluffy pillows as she watched him search his pockets for a condom. Her blood began to cool as she suddenly remembered that she was tired.

"Shit!" Bodega muttered.

Reese's eyes drifted shut. At last she'd made it to her nice, soft bed.

"Reese?" Bodega's incredulous voice sounded in the soft darkness stealing over her.

She was too far gone to answer. His lips brushed hers and she heard him turn to leave just before the darkness of sleep claimed her.

Several hours later the alarm went off. Reese shut it off and sat up in the early morning light. Her clothes were rumpled and several buttons were undone on her top, but she still had on all her clothes. She remembered letting Bodega into her room and allowing him to kiss and touch her. Hell, she'd kissed and touched him too. Too bad she didn't remember much. The first time any man had touched her in months and she'd fallen asleep. She wanted to laugh out loud, but there was no quashing her thoughts that insisted she'd copped out on purpose to avoid cheating on Nick.

Throwing the covers back, she padded into the bathroom and began her morning routine. Today they would hear about the security system and determine how they were going to get past it without being detected. Afterward, she would have enough information to start forming her plan to get the virus away from Barkley and his crew. She couldn't share her information with Flaherty because Barkley had sequestered the team to the other side of the compound and she hadn't been able to remove the pickup units she'd planted on the other side of the facility. Her comm and the earrings were now too far away from the pickup units to transmit anything. She tried to get back to the other side on early morning and evening runs, but security was too tight to risk everything.

Nick spent the morning setting up his office at CIA headquarters and doing a survey of the locked files on the computer system. He had a monumental task ahead, but he was up to the challenge.

Raven Ramone, the partner he'd had before the agency teamed him with Reese, dropped by to welcome him back, dressed in a tight-fitting outfit that showed all her curves. He knew Raven wanted him, but he wasn't interested. Their personal history had ended long before Reese came along, but with rumors circulating about a divorce, Raven seemed ready to renew their relationship. Nick took the time to assure her that there would be no divorce.

By the time Nick arrived at the briefing room, Flaherty was at the media console, but he'd finished loading the mission data.

Nick stared at him critically. People didn't last long in positions like his because of the stress, but the man hadn't cracked.

Flaherty turned to face him. Nick saw that he wasn't wearing his Superman tie, the one he always wore when he sent Nick on the most challenging jobs. This time, a Spider-Man caricature crawled down the front of Flaherty's tie. Perhaps that meant the project would take a lot of skill and ingenuity, he mused.

"Welcome back, Nick," Flaherty said as Nick entered the briefing room.

"It's good to be back." Nick took a seat at one of the gray modular workstations and switched on the computer. He found himself wondering which tie Flaherty had worn when he'd sent Reese on her assignment. Settling down, he noted that Raven was already seated across from him.

Flaherty faced them with two folders in his hands. "Raven, this assignment will exercise your detection skills and Nick's talent for strategy and breaking into high-end security systems. With Reese out of the loop on assignment, I thought the two of you could work together."

Nick and Raven nodded and accepted the briefing packages.

Flaherty seemed pleased as he clicked the first chart onto the screen—a massive, high-tech gun with a huge battery pack. "The U.S. Air Force laboratory has been working to build what they call a Lightning Gun. The weapon operates on the same principles as lightning, but on a much larger scale. It's actually a high-power microwave device that can fuse the electronics on enemy weapons and devices with millions of watts of power. The plans were stolen yesterday. We're pretty sure that a man by the name of Eric Rhineweld has them."

Nick squeezed his fist in frustration. So Flaherty was sending him on a mission that had nothing to do with Reese. He'd do the job to prove to Flaherty he was still one of the CIA's top operatives. But when he returned, the ball would be back in his court and he would demand answers about Reese.

With the little recorder and the extra storage disks nearly full with data she couldn't transmit, Reese began to get desperate. If something happened to her, the CIA would not get the information needed to stop Barkley. She had to do something to retrieve at least one of her pickup units.

The answer came to her one night when she took her earrings off to give her earlobes a break. She would tell Barkley that she just had to go back to her room on the other side for some personal items. If he wanted specifics, she would stress personal-care items only a woman would use. He would probably send a guard to watch her, but she would have a chance to get one of the pickup units. If that didn't work, she'd form Plan B.

At breakfast the next morning she sat at the table she usually shared with Barkley and Bodega in the dining room. Sunlight streamed in from the window. A few team members sat drinking coffee or fixing breakfast, but it was still early.

She greeted Barkley when he set a plate full of ham and eggs on her table and took a seat. As he went back for coffee, she rehearsed mentally. Should she just come out with her request, or ask for a favor? She hated the thought of being in debt to Barkley for anything.

He came back to the table sipping a mug of black coffee and rubbing at sleep-filled eyes. "I'll be glad when we've finished this project," he growled. "The late nights and early mornings are killing me."

"You're the boss," she said lightly, her lips forming a smile.

"Yeah, and I'm going to take all the steps we need beforehand to make sure we hit our target and get out as quickly as possible. If it means I don't get much sleep till it's over, I'll handle it, but I sure as hell don't like it." He guzzled more coffee and looked down at his plate.

She took a deep breath and blurted it out, "I need to go back to my quarters on the other side for some personal things."

His head came up and the stare he leveled at her was full of questions. "Like what?"

Reminding herself that she couldn't give him

any inconsistent or guilty behavior to zero in on, she met his eyes calmly. "Like a book, the cross my mother gave me that I lost somewhere in the room, and things that only a woman would use. You want an itemized list?" she asked in a voice that straddled the line between good-natured insolence and giving Barkley the respect he was due.

He grinned at that. "Nah, but I'll send a guard with you. You don't talk to anyone but him, understand?"

"Yes, I wouldn't think of it."

"And get everything you need this time, because we're almost ready to go on this one."

Reese felt some of her tension ease. "When can I go?"

He checked his watch. "It's only a little after seven. If you hurry, you can do it now. You're not briefing the team this morning and we're not going to start till eight."

"I'll run to my room and get the key," she said, standing.

Barkley was the only person in camp allowed to use a cell phone. He drew it from his pocket, punched in a number and placed it on his ear. "I'll have the guard meet you outside the mess hall."

"Okay." Turning, she headed for her room at a

brisk pace. At the mess hall entrance she nearly ran into Bodega.

His shiny, black hair still looked wet from his morning shower. The depths of his ebony eyes warmed at the sight of her and his sensual mouth formed a smile.

"Good morning," she managed to say in a voice that sounded almost normal.

He echoed her greeting. "You've already had breakfast?" Disappointment filled his tone.

It was hard to keep herself from returning his smile. "Yeah. I've got to run an errand, but I'll be back before the meeting starts."

"Then I'll see you later." He moved out of her path to get a plate from the stand alongside the wall.

Reese noticed then that they were being watched by a couple of people. She hurried to her quarters.

Minutes later, with the key in her pocket, she climbed into the shiny black car the guards used for patrols and saw the driver was Eddy. She'd seen the guard several times around the camp since she'd arrived there. He'd always said hello to her.

He greeted her and turned to fill the car with the sounds of Eminem. At the high, sliding electric gate separating the two sides of camp, she told them where she was going.

Reese took in the activity on the other side of the camp as they passed through the gate and continued on. Groups of recruits jogged through the crisp morning air in formation. Some people performed group exercises on the damp grass.

Outside the mess hall she caught sight of Larry, peeling vegetables. Had he seen her? She couldn't tell because he wore dark glasses.

At the dorm Eddy followed her to her old room. Using her key, she opened her door, her fingers fiddling with her earrings as though they were irritating her earlobes. The room was as she'd left it, but stuffy.

Leaving the guard to lounge in the doorway, she opened the window. Her pickup unit was still on a limb outside her room, hidden by the leaves. "Sorry, it's stuffy in here," she mumbled, half to the guard and half to see if Flaherty was listening.

Eddy bobbed his head up and down.

Flaherty's voice sounded in her ear as she bent down and pretended to search under the bed. "Reese, we haven't heard from you in more than a week. Are you okay?"

"Yes," she murmured.

Flaherty continued. "Last time we talked they were taking you to a different area to work with Barkley's project team. I'm assuming that you didn't get a chance to move the pickup units."

"Hmm," she managed to say, making it sound affirmative.

"We're receiving the playback from all the information you've gathered. Can you talk?"

"No," she said coming out from beneath the bed.

Reese made a big production of continuing her search. She looked in each of her dresser drawers.

"I'm going to check the bathroom," she said, heading toward it.

The guard didn't bother to respond.

Reese guessed that his major concern was preventing her from talking to anyone. Away from him, she made noise with the cabinets and drawers and spoke to Flaherty with her comm. "I'm staying as long as I can to play back the most important information," she told him. "But we have a meeting at eight. I have a guard watching in my quarters, so retrieving the pickup unit is going to be risky."

"Maybe you shouldn't risk it,' Flaherty said. "We can have Larry retrieve them."

"I can do this," she said, slamming shut the medicine chest door.

"Okay," Flaherty conceded in a flat voice.

"If you don't get all the info, just know that he is concentrating on the labs run by the Viper terrorist group, specifically the ones in South America and Central America."

"Larry's going to make a run on Barkley's quarters tomorrow night," Flaherty said.

Before she could respond, Reese heard a noise behind her. Her heart raced as she whipped around to find the guard in the doorway.

"I thought I heard you talking to someone," he said.

"No." She didn't bother to explain. Reese moved aside in a silent challenge.

The guard charged past her to scan the tiny room, checking the closet and beneath the sink. He found nothing unusual. "Just doing my job," he muttered.

"I'm done in here. I must have brought my allergy pills with me, because they aren't here." She moved back into her bedroom. He followed on her heels.

"I think I worked up a sweat," she remarked, crossing the room to stand in front of the open window. In a move born of pure bravado, she slid the screen upward, leaned out of the window and stretched, her arms going wide. On both sides, her fingers touched and disappeared into the leafy branches of the tree. As soon as she felt the cold metal and plastic of the pickup unit, she palmed it and pulled her arms back.

She ducked her head back into the room and caught the guard staring at her big butt. Her natural distraction? Thrilled with her success, she suppressed a smile. "I can't wait to get back outside."

She closed and locked the window. Blocking the guard's vision with her body, she slipped the unit into her pants pocket. Then, she took a box of cookies she'd left on her desk and dropped it into her bag. She also grabbed her copies of *New Weapons for the 21st Century* and *One Hundred Ways to Foil a Sneak Attack.*

"We're going to have to hurry back," she said as she headed for the door.

Larry was standing in the yard when they passed the mess hall. Reese was certain he saw the thumbs-up she gave him as she rested against the outside of the car.

She wanted him to know she'd been successful in getting the comm unit. She knew that Flaherty would fill him in on their discussion.

As she and Eddy returned through the gates to

the other side of the facility, she relaxed a little. Now that she had the pickup unit, she would be able to communicate with Flaherty again. Her mind went to work on the best time and place to plant the pickup unit without looking suspicious. No easy task with the amount of security Barkley had on the team.

Chapter 6

Dressed in white coveralls with the name of an alarm company emblazoned on the back, Nick and Raven stood outside Rhineweld's private villa in Marseilles, France and rang the bell. It had taken Raven exactly two days to locate Rhineweld.

Nick had gathered the intel about the alarm company and the alarm system. Then he'd gotten his special equipment through his contacts in France. Once Rhineweld left the house, Nick used some of the equipment and his knowledge of the frequency used by Rhineweld's wireless

home alarm system to cause a number of intermittent false alarms. Eventually, the frustrated
housekeeper called the alarm company. Nick and
Raven intercepted that call.

The fancy white door to the villa opened. An
older woman with soft blue eyes and graying
blond hair stood in a blue dress and frilly white
apron, filling the entrance. Introducing herself as
an alarm company representative, Raven spoke
French, punctuating her speech with gestures and
a smile.

Stepping to the side, the woman welcomed
them in. Nick followed Raven inside with their
equipment. He set the cases down on the expen-
sive-looking rug covering most of the hardwood
floor in the enormous, high-ceilinged hall. He
looked around and realized Rhineweld had done
all right for himself. There was even a small Re-
noir, or a damn good copy, on the wall in the for-
mal entrance. This place and its furnishings
screamed money.

The consummate professional, Raven cau-
tioned the woman to warn everyone in the villa
that the alarm system was being serviced and that
no one should open any doors or windows. The
woman quickly assured them that there was no
one else in the house to worry about.

Raven drew a card and a small spray bottle from her purse. She gave the housekeeper the card and a face full of spray. Startled, the woman stepped back, holding her hands up and coughing hard. Then she stumbled and started to fall. Nick was holding his breath when he caught her and laid her unconscious form on the couch in the living room. She would be out for at least a couple of hours.

With the housekeeper out of the way, Nick and Raven went to work, looking for the safe. First they tried the most probable areas, like the study and the master bedroom. In each room, they knocked on the walls to reveal hollow areas and search for hidden mechanisms.

In Rhineweld's study, Nick hit the jackpot when he pushed and pressed on the paneling along one wall. The paneling slid back noiselessly to reveal a tunnel.

At the end of the tunnel was the expensive Gold Box brand safe he'd brought the tools to open. Leading to the end of the tunnel was a series of light beams and photoelectric sensors that would detect his entry and trigger an alarm or some sort of countermeasure. Using his flashlight and spotting several small holes, Nick guessed that it was gas. He'd seen this alarm and gas intruder repellent set up in other missions he'd performed for the CIA.

There was no sign of the control panel or any wiring. For a couple of precious minutes, he toyed with the idea of using one of the saws in one of his cases to open up the wall near the alarm system and get at the control box. Somehow he didn't think Rhineweld would have made it that easy for him.

It had been a long time since Nick had had to break in the hard way. With a sigh of resignation, he withdrew a device that looked like a gun from the case and snapped in a stake threaded through with strong cording. Donning his safety glasses, he shot the spike into the high ceiling above the matrix of light beams and sensors. It tore through the thin metallic ceiling and embedded itself securely. He shot another spike into the wall near the opening, for anchoring his rope.

Raven cleared one of bookshelves and dragged it close.

Nick was almost smiling as he climbed the bookshelf and attached his harness and the pulley system. Soon he was hanging in the air above the sensors and dropping down lightly, right in front of the safe.

"I'll go check on the housekeeper and look

out for Rhineweld," Raven said as soon as she saw that he'd made it.

It took a lot of time and maneuvering with his arms at unnatural angles, but he finally managed to get his safecracking device out of his backpack and attach it to the safe. Five minutes later, he heard a *click* and opened the safe. The plans for the Lightning Gun were on top of the pile. Nick put it in a waterproof bag and stowed it in his pack.

By the time Raven came back, he was high above the sensors again, working his way back. As soon as he was back on solid ground, they packed up their equipment and took off.

Back at their small, quaint hotel, they called in their find. The authorities would be picking up Rhineweld immediately. While Nick packed their bags, Raven made reservations for the flight home. With a couple of hours to kill, they stopped to eat in a cozy little restaurant.

"We're still a good team, Nick," Raven murmured as she leaned close to touch his hand.

Nick was silent. He had nothing to say. Being with Raven only made him think of Reese and how much he missed her. He filled his mouth with more of the house specialty, coq au vin. He might as well have been eating cardboard.

"You're pretty quiet," Raven remarked, making an obvious effort to get him to talk. "Do you miss her that much?"

Nick's gaze met hers. "Yes, I do."

"It's not as if you could see her right now, anyway. She's on assignment." Raven looked uncomfortable.

"I'd feel better if I knew where she was and the type of assignment she was on." He studied Raven, trying to figure out why she was so ill at ease. It wasn't just because she'd decided she'd like to jump his bones after all these years and he'd declined.

He watched her try not to swill her wine. It was something she did when she was nervous. Nick dropped the fork onto his plate. Damn it, she knew something.

"Do you know something about Reese's mission?"

"What makes you think that?" Raven asked coolly. She almost had herself under control.

"I know you and I know when you're hiding something!" His tone was rough. "Now tell me what you know."

Raven was quiet, several expressions coloring her face and then disappearing. "You can't run with this," she said. "I've been working backup and support on this one, and Flaherty has already reminded me about keeping my mouth shut."

"Cut the bull, I'm a big boy."

Raven's eyes went soft and sympathetic. "I don't know what the original mission was, but she's with a paramilitary group in Michigan that's going after a virus. She's got to either destroy it or get it back into government hands, and it's one that's worse than that Ebola virus."

Nick's grip tightened on his water glass. It took every bit of his concentration to release the glass before he crushed it in his hand. "Who's the partner?" he asked, wondering if they'd given Reese someone who could hold his own.

"Some FBI guy new to our cell. It's a joint mission, and I heard he's good."

His stomach rumbled. He knew that Reese was one of the best at what she did, but he was almost sorry he'd asked about her assignment. Knowing that things would have been different if he'd been around rankled. He tossed some money on the table and stood.

"We should get on to the airport."

Raven stood with her purse and grabbed his hand. "It'll work out."

Reese sat in the meeting room with the other members of the team, debating various methods of entering either of the two Viper labs, taking it over, and securing the virus and hopefully the cure. Barkley had sent advance scouts, Mick and Carlos, to watch each lab and the traffic in and out. The team had already spent a couple of hours watching the highlights of the surveillance tapes from the scouts.

There was enough testosterone in the room to fuel a football team. Tired of the endless grandstanding and suggestions that never went anywhere, Reese finally stood and took a green dry-erase marker to the whiteboard. She wasn't going to die on this mission, and that meant making sure they succeeded, whether she liked it or not. The group fell silent as she used a marker to divide the board into sections. "Let's get all the information down so we can make the best decision."

"I think we should enter with the truck that services the cafeteria," Bodega said. "There aren't any cameras there and it's centrally located."

Without turning to look at him, Reese wrote his idea in one block and his comment under pros.

"We can do better than that," Walters said sarcastically. "If we go in that way, you can't neutralize the security system without them seeing you. We could put a few of us on the cleaning crew, neutralize the alarm system, and then let every-one in."

Reese wrote that on the board and turned back to the group. Barkley was staring at her with heat in his eyes. She wanted to puke. She resisted the urge to check and make sure the top buttons on her blouse were fastened.

"Why not pay an employee with access to the security database to put us in the system tempo-rarily, pictures and all?" Morrison asked.

"Too risky," Barkley said.

In the middle of writing, Reese turned to face Barkley. She wished she could transmit all the planning information she'd been getting back to Flaherty. Her comm had been silent ever since the team moved to the new area. She wasn't sure if the pickup unit she'd replanted was working.

"Any other ideas?" she asked.

There were a couple more. Everyone scanned the list for several moments, then they took a vote. By the time they broke for dinner, the group had decided that a couple of them would go in on the cleaning crew.

Food that had been sent over from the mess hall sat in plastic containers on the main table, along with forks, spoons, plates and cups. There was a microwave oven on another table for warming food. A few of the other team members sat at another table.

Luckily, the food was still warm. Reese filled her plate and took a seat at one of the tables. Bodega and Barkley got their food and followed her to the table.

"Things are going great. I couldn't ask for much more," Barkley declared as he lifted his fork and began to eat.

Reese chewed and swallowed. "Between nailing down the details and practicing, we should be ready in a week."

"The timing on the security system and its tie into the individual labs is going to be the thing," Bodega put in. "If we don't do this just right, we end up trapped in the lab and exposed to the virus."

Reese's stomach tightened. She knew the risks, yeah, but having Bodega point them out made her nervous. Her plan to get the virus from Barkley was only beginning to form in her mind.

Bodega's warm hand touched hers briefly beneath the table. Was he trying to comfort her, or cop a feel? She didn't dare look at him. Instead she faced Barkley, finished her food and listened as he rambled on about a set of Jet Li movies he'd gotten in the mail.

"It'll be a good way to relax. You could come by and watch them with me tonight," Barkley said, flashing the pearly whites in a manner that no doubt had caused many a heart to flutter.

Startled, she could only stare at him. Underneath the table, Bodega was moving his thumb and forefinger up and down her index finger in a parody of the act. Was he trying to clue her in on Barkley's suggestion or was he making a suggestion of his own?

Firmly pulling her hand away, she said, "Actually, I'm pretty tired. I was up late last night for the project and I was up early this morning to exercise. Can I take a rain check?"

"Anytime." The light in Barkley's eyes promised much more than a movie, if she ever decided to take him up on it.

Bodega rose. "I'll see you both tomorrow. I've got some more specs on the security system to check, and then I'll say good-night."

"Good night." Reese and Barkley spoke in unison.

Reese quickly realized that she'd made a tactical error. She should have left before Bodega. Barkley was eyeing her with renewed speculation.

Behind Barkley, Derrick Stack was approaching the table with a plate of food. He was as new to the team as she was, so his background had not been in Flaherty's files. Reese focused on him.

"Mind if I sit down?" Stack asked Barkley when he made it to the table. "I have something I want to discuss with you."

Seizing the opportunity to make her escape, Reese stood and yawned. There was a silver-colored room key in her chair. She examined it for a moment, wondering how it had fallen out of her pocket.

Far from being deep in a conversation with Stack, Barkley was eyeing her. "Anything wrong?"

"No." She yawned again for emphasis. "I think I'll turn in."

Barkley turned to Stack. "Is this something she needs to hear?"

Stack looked uncertain. "I thought I'd see what you thought before I tried it out on the group."

Barkley nodded a bit regretfully. "Fine." He turned back to Reese. "Good night."

"Good night," she echoed, then made her escape. As she left the area, she made the observation that most of the team, with the exception of Barkley and Morrison, were still eating. The hall leading to the rooms was deserted.

At her door, Reese removed the key she'd found in her chair and fit it into her lock. It wouldn't turn. She reached into her back pocket and found her real key. So it wasn't her key after all. She'd halfway suspected that it was Bodega's key all along.

So now he was inviting her to his room. Reese wasn't sure she wanted to go. No, she corrected herself, she *did* want to go. But she had a feeling that she shouldn't.

Reese opened her door and entered her room, which seemed small and claustrophobic. Switching on the lights, she locked the door. This was the perfect time to work on her plan. She sat at her desk and paged through the folders and pictures, trying to make it all come together.

Finally pushing the stack aside, she covered her face with her hands. A provocative picture of Bodega waiting in bed for her kept insinuating itself into her thoughts. It had been much too long since she'd had any sexual satisfaction. Her body ached, begging her to make her fantasy real.

She stood with the key in her hand and took a couple of steps toward the door. No. She didn't need any distractions right now. Flinging the key onto the desk, Reese made her way into the bathroom to shower.

Minutes later, feeling refreshed and more focused after the shower, Reese went through her
nightly routine and pulled on a cotton nightgown.
She'd just settled back at her desk when she heard
a light tapping on her door. Drawing her SIG, she
went to answer it.

Through the peephole, she spotted Bodega. The
hot, wild feeling came back with a vengeance.
Flicking the lock and turning the knob, she opened
the door. He stood in the doorway in a tank and
shorts that bared much of his muscular, bronze
body and sent her imagination spinning out of
control.

"May I come in?"

Nodding, she stepped aside, her nostrils filling
with the scent of fresh soap as he passed. She
closed the door behind him.

"Did you find my key?" he asked, standing
close enough for her to feel the heat of his body.

"Yes." She hated the breathless sound of her
voice.

His eyes were hot and mesmerizing. "After the
other day, I haven't been able to get you off my
mind. You said yes. You wanted me, too." His
voice softened. "Did you change your mind?"

Swallowing, she leaned back against the door.
She wasn't going to lie about this. "No, not really."

Bodega thrust his hand into her hair, pushing it back gently and sending a shiver of anticipation through her.

"But you didn't use the key."

"I couldn't. There's a lot going on...."

"This has nothing to do with the project," he said firmly. "This is between you and me. It can mean as much or as little as *we* decide."

His warm lips brushed hers once, twice. She smelled the mint on his breath. Then those dark eyes were staring into hers, trying to learn her secrets.

"You're married," he guessed.

"Going through a divorce," she confessed.

He cursed softly in Spanish. "I won't push you. You tell me to go away."

"I can't." Reaching out, she pulled him close so that their lips fused in a hard kiss.

He pulled back to caress lips with his tongue before kissing her deeply again. "I prayed you wouldn't send me away," he groaned.

Thrilling, sensual threads of desire shot through her. Her hands wandered his bronzed body, from his muscled chest, to his slim waist, hard butt and strong thighs, verifying that this was not a dream.

His fingers traced the deep vee in the neckline

of her nightgown, drawing it down so his mouth could suck on one aching breast.

Gasping, she curled herself around him, one hand in the midnight-dark waves of his hair, the other holding on to his shoulder for dear life.

"Now, *querida*," he whispered as she undulated against him. His hands pushed the cotton fabric past her thighs to cup her buttocks and lift her up.

Circling his waist with her legs, she allowed him to carry her to the bed. He laid her down on the edge and stood above her open legs. He withdrew a condom from his shorts before slipping them off, then passed it to her. He wore nothing underneath. She reached for his erection with both hands and slid the condom down the swollen length.

His mouth fused with hers once more as he laid her back, his body covering hers and his hand moving restlessly between her thighs. His kisses turned deeper and move provocative.

Suddenly Reese sat up, pushing him away. Tears filled her eyes. "I can't do this!"

For several moments there was only the sound of his harsh breathing. He turned away from her, struggling to control himself. "I never thought you would be one to play games."

"I'm not playing games." She wiped away the tears with a fierce, angry movement. This was not the time to show weakness.

He stood and began to gather his clothes. She made a point of not watching, but the rustling sounds he was making putting on his clothes suddenly stopped.

"Why, *querida*?"

She looked up to see that he'd already donned his shorts. His gaze burned her. "I'm not ready," she said simply. "I can't do this until it feels right for me."

She found the silver key and dropped it into his palm. "Good night, Arturo."

He stared at her silently, his eyes making an eloquent plea. Then he echoed her words and added in a voice that vibrated right through her, "Sweet dreams."

As soon as the door shut behind him she locked it and shoved a chair beneath it. Was she keeping Bodega out, or keeping herself in? She wouldn't let herself think about it.

She felt hot, achy and irritable as she got ready for bed. Bodega was all man and not one to be put off or ignored for long. As she climbed between the sheets, she assured herself that she could handle him—and the looming mission ahead.

Chapter 7

Something unusual snatched Reese from a warm, comforting sleep. She didn't know what, but her eyes opened to inky darkness and she listened to the noises outside her door. Several people were moving around in the hall, trying to be quiet.

Paranoid and cursing under her breath, Reese threw back the covers and got out of bed, her SIG already in her hand. She drew on her robe and stepped into her house shoes, suddenly awake and intent on investigating.

Outside her door with guns drawn, Barkley's

guards fanned out to fill the hall outside all the doors.

The last vestiges of sleep disappeared. She took an involuntary step back from the door, forcing herself to breathe while she evaluated her options. She could defend herself with her guns and knives, she reasoned, but a lone agent against a group of steely-eyed killers and thugs? At least she'd go out in a blaze of glory.

But if they knew she was CIA, they'd be in her room now, trying to make her talk. Visually and mentally checking the room for things that might give her away, she reactivated the comm. Flaherty's voice filled her ears.

"Reese, where have you been?"

Knowing better than to confess that she'd switched off the comm when she'd been with Bodega, she kept her answer short. "Asleep until some kind of commotion started in the hall. Barkley's guards are out there, guns drawn."

"Yes, well he's probably on a witch hunt. We've been trying to contact you and warn you. They caught Larry in Barkley's quarters."

Reese's head snapped up, her stomach sinking. *Dear Lord, not Larry, too.* Did she need to mount a rescue? "No! Is he—?"

"Larry's okay for now. He escaped the facility and we have a team on the way to pick him up."

She scanned the room, back to looking for anything Barkley might find suspicious. She didn't dare destroy the video-camera earrings she'd been wearing every day, but the miniature recorder and its cable were giveaways. Wrapping the cable around the little radio and headphones she used when she jogged, she stared at the recorder. What could she do with it?

"Reese? You still there?" Flaherty sounded concerned.

She answered, intent on reassuring him. "I'm still here, just trying to find something to do with the recorder before they search this room. I'm turning off the comm now and won't turn it on again unless it's absolutely necessary."

"You have the pickup information. Contact us when you can. Flaherty out."

"Yes, sir. Whittaker out." Switching off the comm, she took a deep breath and let it out slowly. Adrenaline shot through her veins. She focused on the ceiling tiles, her bed and the computer desk. All were places she knew they'd look.

Outside the rooms, a loudspeaker flared to life. "Team, this is Barkley. We have discovered an emergency situation. I need everyone to meet me out in the hall ASAP. I repeat, this is an emergency."

Not worrying about changing back into her fatigues, she knew that her robe and V-neck sleep shirt would give her the advantage with Barkley.

In a burst of inspired desperation, she emptied the open box of chocolate chip cookies that had been her willpower challenge to herself onto a plate, put the recorder on the bottom and replaced half the cookies. It would have to do.

Through the connecting wall, she heard Bodega moving around his quarters. Briefly she wondered if he, too, was getting rid of something suspicious. She liked him a lot, and was hoping maybe he wasn't at the facility to go along with Barkley's program.

She broke most of the extra cookies into bits and flushed them down the toilet. Hearing the sounds of the guards slamming beefy fists against the doors in the corridor, she hurried, washing her hands.

Then the knocking at her door was lighter, with a calmer edge. *Barkley.*

Stepping back into the room, she opened the door, the box of cookies in her hand. Barkley stood in the entrance, his gaze meeting hers, then falling to peruse her cleavage, laid bare by her nightgown. Her skin crawled, but she managed to turn her lips up in a semblance of a smile.

Raw lust and admiration gleamed in his sea-green eyes. "Reese, I swear you're wasted in those fatigues you like to wear. Lady, you are some piece of work."

She resisted the urge to pull the robe tight to cover her cleavage. It would only define her curves and give him more to look at. "Is this the emergency situation?" she asked in a light tone, intent on bringing his mind back to business. Behind him, she saw that some of the other team members were already standing in the corridor. Some wore pajama bottoms and shorts. Bodega stood on the fringe in jeans, his magnificent chest bare; he was talking to one of the others.

"No, *this* is not the emergency situation." Barkley's gaze turned serious as he stepped aside. "This is about business, so join the others out in the hall. This is going to take a while."

"Any objections to my taking a snack?" she asked, proffering the box of cookies.

"No," he said, extending a hand.

Reese went still inside and gave him the box.

"Chocolate chip is my favorite," he said, reaching in to grab a couple. Thanks." He returned the box.

"You're welcome." She made herself relax as she left her room to join the others.

Barkley gestured, and two of the guards stepped forward and entered her room.

"What's going on?" she asked, her voice indignant. "Do you think I took something?"

"No. We have to search everyone's room. I'm going to explain everything," he promised, turning away. "We're meeting in the cafeteria. Now."

Conscious of the hungry looks she was getting from the men, she followed, wondering if keeping the outfit on to distract Barkley had been worth it. She'd probably lost a few points on the macho scale they measured everybody against and had made it to the top of the one for eye candy. Shrugging inwardly, she decided that she'd just have to kick more butt.

In the pleasantly cool night air, they left the dorm to cross the path to the small cafeteria. There, more guards waited to take each person into the back to be searched. Barkley explained that Lana had discovered someone in a restricted area and had been shot and killed by the perpetrator. The perpetrator had escaped, but the incident highlighted that there might be accomplices or spies in the facility, and possibly on Barkley's project team. Tonight's actions were Barkley's way of dealing with the situation.

She knew that Larry had ventured into Barkley's quarters. She could imagine Lana going after him.

Reese sat with the team in the dining hall. As the number of people in the group dwindled, she felt anger building at the thought of Barkley sending a couple of his goons to strip-search her with a bunch of men. She wasn't having it. By the time it was her turn to be escorted to the room in the back, she could have burned him with her gaze. She went quietly, but was ready to raise hell if she had to.

The door opened to the room they were using for searches and Walters stepped out, giving her a menacing look. Yeah, he still had plans for her. Glaring at him, she entered the room and got a surprise. One of the nurses from the clinic stood behind the curtain in her uniform, nodding.

"Just take everything off, let me examine you and your clothing, and we'll be done," she said in a businesslike manner.

Reese did as the woman asked, glad Flaherty hadn't insisted that she wear a wire or anything obvious. There was still something degrading about having to strip on command and being inspected like a piece of meat. Gritting her teeth, she tried to get it over with. She had one touchy moment when the nurse flicked the video camera earrings in her fingers and commented, "Nice earrings."

Then she was done.

Back in the cafeteria, the staff had opened the kitchen to serve coffee, juice and pastries. Reese stifled a groan when she saw that the only open spot was between Bodega and Barkley. They'd saved her a seat.

Both men watched her walk over to the table. Bodega's liquid eyes held a watered-down hint of the hot caressing looks he gave her behind closed doors. Barkley was simply drooling, his sharp eyes clinging to her every curve.

Pretending to ignore the obvious, she settled in the empty chair between them. "So what's the verdict?" she asked Barkley.

"So far, everyone is clean," he answered. "We've finished the personal searches and we're almost done with the rooms. Then I'll make an announcement, and everyone who wants to can get back to bed."

"Those who aren't swilling down coffee," she remarked.

"I saved you some cookies." Barkley chuckled, sliding the box across the table at her.

"Thanks." Holding it, Reese noticed that the box felt much lighter. She wondered if Barkley had found the recorder and was simply playing along. Placing it on the table, she resisted the urge to check to see if the recorder was still inside. "I'm going to get some decaf. Anyone else?"

Both men said no.

Half an hour later, still sipping her decaf at the table, Reese heard Barkley announce that nothing concrete or suspicious had been found in any of the searches and thank everyone for their patience.

Just as everyone prepared to return to their rooms, Barkley threw a new monkey wrench into all their plans. He announced that having spies at his facility made him nervous, so he was moving up the date when the team would take the Viper lab, to within three days.

Reese knew this would impact on Flaherty's plans. With the box of cookies in her hands, she strode back to the dorm flanked by Barkley and Bodega. By the time she made it inside her room, her head pounded mercilessly.

With the door closed, she checked the cookie

box and found the recorder intact on the bottom. She breathed a sigh of relief. It would be a while before she could contact Flaherty, because of the bugs Barkley's guards may have planted in her room.

With the checking done and the CD player pumping jazz in the background, she contacted Flaherty and broke the news. His voice turned low and edgy. This new development jeopardized his plans to send in an agency team to scoop up the virus before Barkley's team did, using information he'd gotten from Reese.

Certain she could secure the virus for the government, Reese didn't see a problem. "Don't you think I can get the virus from the team and bring it back to the agency?" she asked, feeling that her abilities were being questioned. He'd ordered her to join Barkley's special team and then let Larry try for the codes. Now it looked as if she wouldn't even get the chance to secure the virus, despite all the undercover work she'd done at Barkleyville. Next he would be telling her that she couldn't bring Barkley in.

Flaherty refused to bend. "It's not about your abilities, Reese, it's about maximizing our opportunities to bust Barkley and the terrorist ring."

"So what's Barkley going to think when we get

there and there's no virus?" she argued. "He's going to suspect his team of betraying him."

"He'll probably think he got scooped by someone in the business or suspect the good doctor of double-crossing him," Flaherty replied. "Besides, you excel at this kind of thing. I'm sure you could convince him of whatever is necessary."

Reese clenched her fists. She could take orders, but she didn't have to like them. "Is there anything I can do to get you to change your mind?"

"No, Reese, but when you get back from the mission I want you to make a run on the stolen code."

Reese went still. This was a new development. "You mean Larry didn't get the code?"

"No," he answered in an even tone. "But he thinks he found a secret room. We've already picked him up, so I'll let him explain everything."

Larry got on the comm and filled her in. After listening carefully and saying goodbye, Reese climbed into bed exhausted. The risk in their plan had just gone up another notch.

Chapter 8

Bodega's rich voice washed over Reese in warm currents as he briefed the team assembled in the conference room on the Viper labs' automated security systems, the methods he would use to disable them, and the estimated time it would take.

She followed his logic and method, comparing his plans with what she would have done. His presentation merely confirmed what she'd already figured out. Bodega wasn't just a good-looking fighting machine. He had a sharp mind that she couldn't help but admire.

She listened, somewhat amused, as members of the group peppered him with questions. What if the security equipment at the lab was a different make or model? What if there was a backup system he didn't know about?

Bodega kept his cool, his jaw tightening only minutely. He dealt with each question, tearing it apart in terms of the likelihood of it happening, and the impact it could have on their mission. Without giving too much of his past away, he revealed that he'd worked for one of the largest security companies in South America.

When he finished, she thought he'd earned a round of applause for a job well done, but it was a shame to see so much skill and talent directed at something so evil. She gave him a professional nod of approval.

Acknowledging it and Barkley's appreciative "good job," Bodega gathered his materials and took a seat near the front.

Watching him unobtrusively, Reese wondered what Bodega was really doing in the camp. She'd been puzzling over that question since she'd met him, because her gut told her he was a good person. She just couldn't believe that he was as corrupt and demented as the rest of the team.

When the group took a ten-minute break and

most of the guys hovered around the coffee, she walked outside to get some fresh air. Settling on the wrought-iron bench beneath an oak tree, she relaxed in the heat of the sunlight and thought about the job.

If she was with Barkley and Bodega when she secured the virus, she would have to kill or disable both of them. The thought of taking Barkley out in the line of duty appealed to her, but she cringed at the idea of eliminating Bodega. Her best chance lay in getting separated from the entire team. Then she could take the Rage virus for the agency and substitute another for Barkley. He wouldn't know the difference until it was too late to do anything about it.

Stretching, Reese made the mistake of looking up into the leafy branches of the tree. The branches formed a notch big enough for two kids to sit comfortably, reminding her of the oak tree in her grandmother's backyard, where she and Riley had spent endless childhood hours.

She blinked and then closed her eyes. A wave of grief slammed into her, throwing her senses off kilter. She dragged trembling fingers across her forehead and back, fighting tears. She wouldn't ever see Riley again...because of an act of senseless violence. The baby was gone, Nick was gone… Her life would never be the same again. She'd lost…everything.

She bit her lips, her fingers pressing deep into her skin. *What are you doing? What are you doing?* The words formed a litany in her mind. This was not the time to fall apart, to give in to the emotions she'd suppressed in order to do her job.

Sounds of approaching footsteps reached her ears. Reese froze, her fingers still on her forehead.

"You okay?" Barkley asked, the bench giving as he sat down beside her.

Not trusting her voice, she slowly shook her head.

"I get migraines too, every now and then," he confided as a bag crackled and he popped something into his mouth and crunched noisily. "Sometimes they last for several days and I'm not good for anything but the bed." His voice took on an ominous note. "Are you going to be able to do the job?"

Reese cleared her throat forcefully and dropped her hands to face him head-on. "I have a simple headache, not a migraine. I'll be able to do the job."

"Good. Want a painkiller or something? I've got some in my quarters." He punctuated his comment with an engaging grin. Lately, he seemed to take it for granted that she would end up in his bed eventually.

"Thanks, but no. I'll be fine," she said, maintaining a bland expression. Reese could just imagine what Barkley's "or something" might be.

"So, do you think we're ready to take the lab?" Barkley asked, changing the subject. The bag in his hand crackled, and she saw him grab another handful of caramel popcorn.

"We've got all the intel we need," she answered honestly, "but I think we need to work on our timeline, smooth everything out, know who's going to be where and when."

Barkley chuckled. "My thoughts exactly. I swear, great minds think alike. After this break we'll spend time working out the timeline I put together based on all the briefings."

Reese managed a grin. She wanted to strangle the psychopath and end this lunacy right then and there. All in due time, she reminded herself.

Glancing down at her watch, she noted the time. "Break's over." She got up from the bench.

"If your head still hurts after this, we're going to get that painkiller," Barkley promised, looking up at her with another grin. "And while you're there, I do a mean massage."

"I bet you do," she quipped, then headed for the building.

Barkley entered after her, retrieved copies of the timeline from the desk and began distributing them.

Head pounding, Reese drew a pen from her pocket and began to mark it up. She was ready to end this mission once and for all.

Shifting restlessly in his leather chair, Nick sat at the desk in his office feeling completely frustrated. He'd pushed the limits of CIA protocol in an attempt to access private information on Reese's assignment. He'd run up against a brick wall. Now, sipping coffee, he made the decision to corner Flaherty again. After all, Reese was still his wife.

This morning he'd awakened with the determination to hop a plane to Michigan to get her. As the day wore on, however, years of training held him back. He might blow her cover and expose her to even more risk.

Tilting the chair back, he switched off the computer screen, but the large red letters were imprinted on his brain: NEW MISSION BRIEFING AT TEN HUNDRED HOURS.

The first thing Nick noticed when he stepped into the briefing room and found Flaherty at the media console was his brightly colored Superman tie. It featured Superman on a blue background, holding his shirt open to expose the red capital *S* emblazoned on his chest.

So that's how it's going to be. Nick greeted Flaherty, acknowledging his response.

"I want you to know that I talked to Reese last night and she was fine," Flaherty said, closing the loading panel.

Nick nodded. His next words were those he always used when his wife was on an assignment without him. "Did she leave me a message?"

"No, she didn't." The look Flaherty shot him held hints of pity.

Nick tensed. It hurt like hell to have Reese just drop him without talking things through first. But he shouldn't have been surprised that she didn't want to talk to him, he reminded himself, no matter how much he wished things were different.

"Tell her that I asked about her."

"Sure." Flaherty's expression was sincere.

"How's Rita?" Nick asked, recovering enough to make small talk.

Evan Flaherty's smile lit his entire face, the way it usually did when he talked about his wife. "She's shopping. We're planning a vacation to New Zealand."

Nick nodded. "That's been on my vacation list for a while."

"Well, maybe you can go after this assignment," Flaherty said. "With all that's happened, you've earned a break from all of this."

With muttered thanks, Nick moved away from him to take a seat at one of the briefing modules. He turned it on.

In the queue were several files with the names and photos of people he'd worked with throughout his years at the agency. He knew that whatever the job was, it would likely require his skills as a security systems expert and his field experience. He knew that Raven excelled at tracking people down, but she also had an awesome knowledge base and experience working with chemical and biological weapons.

Clicking past Raven's file, he saw one for Vince Watts, the resident weapons master and best sniper their cell had to offer, and Blake Peterson, another computer and security systems expert who also excelled at hand-to-hand combat.

At exactly ten o'clock, Flaherty stood to address the group of people that had gathered in the briefing room. "This room is filled with some of the best this Agency has to offer. Most of you have worked together at one time or other. I hope you all have had a chance to look over the information we've pulled from each of your files in support of this mission." He glanced around the room, then continued. "The mission you've been called to execute involves a threat to millions."

The main screen behind him filled with the picture of a large, private laboratory complex. The words Harwell Middlehouse Biotechnology Laboratory, Waikeeno Falls, New Jersey were printed across the bottom.

"This laboratory has developed drugs, vaccines and serums for the U.S. government. Several months ago, one of its scientists illegally acquired samples of a new virus, the Rage virus from Africa, which has killed roughly eighty percent of the people who have come in contact with it. During an accident at the Harwell Middlehouse, all staff who came in contact with it during a laboratory accident died. Laboratory staff lied to government officials about the particular virus involved in the deaths. The virus is missing, and we believe the virus and the scientist working on a cure for it are now in the hands of the terrorist group Viper. Even worse, we have evidence that a paramilitary group is going after the virus."

Nick listened as Flaherty discussed the details

of the assignment. The group Flaherty referred to had to be the one Reese was working under- cover with. Part of him was hoping that it wasn't.

"The paramilitary group is headed by a man named Kevin Barkley, who runs a legitimate weapons and self-defense training camp in Michigan. Our sources tell us he is planning to hit one of the six Viper labs located in South and Central America and retrieve the virus—to sell it to the highest bidder on the black market. A bio- weapon this dangerous cannot end up in the hands of terrorists. Your mission is to determine which lab has the virus and Ballinger, retrieve them, and turn everything over to the government before Barkley and his team can get their hands on them."

Pausing for a moment, Flaherty sipped his cof- fee. "Due to fortuitous planning, we have an agent on Barkley's team who has provided us with all the information he has shared. We have decided not to go in and bust Barkley now, be- cause we have our undercover agent going on the mission with him and have a plan in place in case ours is unsuccessful. We need to get that virus, one way or another. Now, we suspect Barkley is keeping a few details to himself. We'll go over

Barkley's plan to date and form our own. It is my goal for this team to take off for one of the Viper labs in the morning. At this point, the effort is focused on labs in Guatemala and Honduras."

Expecting something of this magnitude and urgency, Nick observed his colleagues in relative calm, noting their surprise. The sooner Flaherty gave them all the information they needed to plan the mission, the better.

"Any questions?" Flaherty stared out at them, ready for a challenge.

Vince Watts spoke up. "Sir, is it possible that we could take another day for planning? With what's at stake, we can't risk failure."

"My thoughts exactly," Flaherty said, not giving an inch. "That's why we can't wait for Barkley's team to get to the virus first. There's also the imminent threat that Viper will come up with the optimum delivery method. I have another team going in to round up every Viper operative we can nab."

The room was silent as everyone digested his words. Flaherty turned off the main screen and signaled the guard at the door. "Before we review the details of Barkley's plans and information, I have asked Dr. Alvin Alvarez to brief you all on handling the virus. I know that some of you have worked with biohazards in the past and I have placed you in lead positions on this team."

At Flaherty's nod, the guard opened the door and a chunky, dark-haired man with a swarthy complexion entered the room. One of the guards followed with a large box. The agents shut off their screens.

"This way, Dr. Alvarez," Flaherty said, gesturing the man to the front of the room. "I've already put your data into the system."

After being formally introduced to the group, Alvarez began his briefing. "I've been told that you have a task that will require you to work with biologically hazardous material in a Biosafety Level 4 facility and that many of you have no experience in this area. This type of facility is designed to prevent infectious microbes from being released into the environment and to provide the highest possible level of safety to scientists carrying out the experiments. I have endeavored to make this lecture as simple as possible. We will go over the basics and then you will all be fitted with a protective suit that we call a 'space suit'."

Nick listened, taking it all in and noting changes in technology and procedures. He'd been on an assignment that involved biohazards with Raven a few years ago. Despite his previous experience, however, he knew they needed more time to plan. Handling the latest bioweapons with the minimal training they were about to receive was risky.

Once Alvarez completed his briefing, Flaherty went back to the media control area to go over the details of the facility and Barkley's plan. He used photos of a three-dimensional model. The pieced-together sections of taped conversations between Barkley and his team came next.

Nick froze at the muffled sound of Reese's voice. He glanced up to find Flaherty watching him and nodding imperceptibly.

So she is involved. Nick forced his attention back to the tape. If both of them had to go after a deadly virus he was glad that he would be first. If something happened to him, at least he would know that Reese was all right.

Chapter 9

Reese woke up early, anxious to get the job done. Her time is Barkley's facility had been more than she bargained for. It was time to get the virus, retrieve the codes, and deal with her life back in the real world.

She massaged the area in front of her ear, but there was nothing from her comm. It had been working intermittently for a day or so. She'd used her earrings to transmit, but hadn't received feedback from the CIA.

In the bathroom, she turned on the shower and checked for bugs. One was embedded in the

smoke alarm. She went back to search the bedroom. It took a while for her to search her computer and its station, the lamps and all the
pictures, but her search netted nothing new. Last
night she had found one in the pencil box on her
desk and had placed it in the little refrigerator.
The only slant she could put on the bugs in her
room was that Barkley didn't really trust her.

Tension was building inside her already, tightening her muscles and making her paranoid. Back
in the bathroom, she took a shower and then
donned her running gear. With her room key in
her pocket, she left the room to tap lightly on
Bodega's door.

His door opened and he stood in the entrance,
dressed only in a pair of white cotton pajama bottoms. Her gaze followed the trail of fine hair
sprinkling his chest to his six-pack and below.
She never tired of looking at Bodega.

Taking her arm, he drew her inside. A sultry
female voice, Hispanic, crooned a love song from
the stereo, and his weights were scattered around
the room.

"What a nice surprise," he said softly, closing
the door carefully. His liquid gaze was hot
enough to melt her clothes off. "Did you come by
for a workout?"

"Yes," she answered, ready to suggest the run she'd dressed for, but she never got the chance.

He stepped forward, backing her into the door. Every inch of his hard, perfectly formed body pressed up against the front of her. She felt his erection poking her stomach, sending sensual waves of desire coursing through her.

"I've been waiting for you for a long time, Reese," Bodega whispered, leaning down to take her mouth in a hot, torrid kiss that weakened her knees.

His expert hands kneaded her buttocks, moving down to her thighs. Despite aching for him, Reese fought for control. They didn't have time to make love. They needed to be sharp and ready for the lab project. Her body might be tempted, but her mind was in charge.

"Stop." Reese pushed against his chest. "We can't do this. We don't have the time—and someone will hear us."

"Now," he said, caressing her face. "Then we will have our memories...if one of us dies."

Leaning back, she gazed into his soulful eyes. She knew then and there that those weren't the eyes of a criminal. She had a feeling that she would soon discover his real motive for working with Barkley.

"We already have a lot of memories—and we'll *both* be coming back from this job."

"Is that a promise?"

"Yes." She believed it, believed they could take the Viper lab and come back with a virus for Barkley. She'd have enough time to retrieve the codes before Barkley discovered the deception. "I need to run and I wanted to do it with you," she continued. "You know, clear my head before we take off."

"Of course. If that's what you want." Hooking his fingers in his waistband, he stripped off his pants right in front of her.

Reese got a provocative close-up of his well-shaped butt, athletic thighs and rock-hard erection. She stared, a warm, shivery sensation settling deep inside her. Seeing him, she felt as if she were somehow being punished. Was he making a point of showing her what she'd turned down? She didn't look away as he pulled on running shorts, a T-shirt, and running shoes and socks. He closed his eyes for a minute and focused inwardly. He had phenomenal control. As Reese watched, his erection disappeared. Then his eyes opened.

"I guess we should hurry," he said, leading her to the door.

They'd just stepped into the passageway and closed the door when another door along the corridor shut noisily. Turning to see who it was, they both tensed.

Barkley stood outside his room, fully dressed, eyes narrowed.

"We were just going for a run," Reese said, trying her best to sound natural. "Would you like to come along?"

For a moment, Barkley regarded them silently, the expression on his face that of someone who'd swallowed something bitter. Then he placed his room key in one pocket and answered. "No, you two go ahead with your run. I'd only get in the way."

Those words carried a double meaning. It took a lot for Reese to avoid Bodega's gaze and school her facial expression so that she didn't look guilty to Barkley. She'd worked hard to keep her relationship with Bodega secret. She and Bodega took their leave and exited the housing building for the crisp morning air and the dirt road that led to the gate separating the two sides of the camp. They had a quarter of a mile under their belts by the time Bodega turned to her and said, "He knows."

Lengthening her stride and establishing a

rhythm, Reese agreed. She was pissed that it was her problem that Barkley had taken a liking to her. Then she was angry with herself for surrendering to Bodega's considerable charm. But she'd been falling apart emotionally and he'd been the perfect no-strings-attached man to catch her. She'd done nothing to lead Barkley on, but to maximize her mission's chances of success, she hadn't totally discouraged him either. Today she would find out just how much depended on his goodwill.

Neither spoke as they reached the gate. After making a hundred-and-eighty-degree turn, they started back.

"We must tread carefully from here, *querida*," Bodega said in a voice barely affected by their brisk pace.

"Yes," Reese agreed, not sure if he was referring to just their relationship.

Chapter 10

When she made it to breakfast, a few scattered team members sat finishing their meals. The atmosphere seemed normal. Looking fresh and energized, Bodega nodded politely as he trekked back to his quarters with a loaded plate.

As she dug into the food, she admitted to herself that she wasn't as confident of the day's success as she'd indicated to Bodega. She savored every bite of her food as if it would be her last.

Walters straggled in late. He surprised Reese by taking a seat at her table. She regarded him warily, the hair on her arms standing up as his lips formed a grimace of a smile.

"Mornin'." His pale gray eyes observed her with an eerie promise in their depths.

"Morning." Her voice came out hard and strong. Sipping her coffee, she waited for him to start something. He'd barely said a word to her since they'd been on this side of the facility, so he had to be up to something.

He chewed noisily, smacking his lips and slurping his coffee, but managed to keep an eye on her.

Finished except for her coffee, she refused to let him ruin her digestion. "Say what you've got to say and get the hell out of my face," she said finally.

That earned her another display of his greasy lips and yellowed teeth. "What did you do? Did the boss catch you servicing the team? Whatever it was, you're off the pedestal!" he declared, cackling with delight.

Surprised, she studied him. He'd seen or heard something that gave him the courage to taunt her. She twisted her face into a mask of disgust. "Walters, I can see that you've lost that last little bit of brains you had. Too bad, 'cause I was saving a bullet for them."

"I saw the boss in the weight room this morning, pummeling the punching bag so hard that I thought it might snap down from the ceiling. He was so pissed, I swear smoke was coming out of his ears, and he kept muttering something over and over. Wanna know what it was?"

Reese's fingers tightened on the coffee cup, tension building inside her. There were a lot of things going on inside and outside of the facility that could piss Barkley off, she told herself. It didn't have to have anything to do with her. He hadn't been happy to see her with Bodega this morning, but Barkley had no way of knowing how far things had gone. Besides, she argued inwardly, he wasn't a man to let personal issues get in the way of the things he wanted to accomplish. Just the same, she wanted to know what he'd said. She nodded as if interested.

Walters' eyes sparkled with malice. "He said, 'You dirty bitch. You damn dirty bitch.' Look around the room. See any other bitches in here?"

Gritting her teeth, she narrowed her eyes and leaned across the table to slowly enunciate each word. "You need to get yourself some business, because one way or another, you're going to stay out of mine. Are we clear?"

His gaze bore into her. "Don't start something you can't finish."

Balling her hand into a fist, Reese whipped it across the table to hit Walters' thorax with her extended knuckle. His eyes widened as his head snapped back. Then he slumped forward, coughing, wheezing and trying to catch his breath. The other team members had stopped eating to watch, but Reese was past caring.

"Want to try me again, you dirty SOB? I won't stop this time until it's over for good."

Walters' eyes shot venom, but he couldn't recover enough to strike back. "Remember what Barkley said," he gasped.

"I remember." She released him suddenly and reclined in her chair. "Make sure you do the same."

"We'll finish this when we get back," he threatened between gasps of air.

"*If* you get back." Reese huffed as she rose and walked away from the table.

Forty minutes later, the team boarded a chartered plane headed for Guatemala City. Reese and Flaherty had assumed Barkley would use this means of transportation. Reese hoped the CIA would be tracking this plane and its destination. She hadn't known which lab they were heading for when the team boarded.

Barkley had reserved the front of the plane for

himself. Reese couldn't interpret his facial expression as she gathered her files with maps and diagrams and invaded his space. This was their last chance to catch anything they might have missed in the planning stages.

"We should go over the plan one more time," she began as she reached his row.

Barkley nodded, the grimmest expression she'd ever seen on his face. "Good idea." He signaled Bodega to join them.

"You seem distracted. What's the problem?" Reese asked when they'd taken adjacent seats in the row with the most legroom.

Barkley gave each of them the eye. "I haven't been able to contact Carlos. He's one of the best and usually checks in with me every couple of days. I think he's been compromised or killed and it's making me nervous. I've put too much time and money into this to lose it now."

Reese and Bodega exchanged a look. A chill ran down Reese's spine, countering the excitement that had begun to bubble when she boarded the plane. Her hands felt cold and clammy. She wondered if their plans had been discovered by Viper. Or maybe the CIA had already acted. Only time would tell.

"We need to go in with one of the backup plans," she said.

Bodega weighed in on her side. "It makes sense to change the plan. We'd have a better chance of success."

Barkley added his agreement, and they studied their packets, discussing contingency plans.

By the time the plane landed, the entire team had been briefed on the changes to the plan, which included taking the lab at night.

Reese stepped off the plane in Guatemala City into air that was surprisingly pleasant: the temperature couldn't have been more than low eighties. She saw that they weren't the only group arriving. Two tour groups of students and adults were already walking into the rectangular terminal building.

Glad to be able to stretch her cramped legs, she followed the groups into the air-conditioned building, the rest of the team on her heels. Inside, she stood in line in front of the team with Bodega and Barkley.

Waiting for her turn with the immigration official, she scanned the crowd, comparing and noting the differences in bone structure, coloring and hair among the natives, and seeing some similarities with Bodega's exotic features. With his Hispanic heritage, he didn't stand out like the tourists and most of the team. Reese knew that with her coloring, she didn't really stand out either. If she had to get away from the team, that would help.

Reese also checked the crowd for people who looked out of place or stood out in the crowd— although she hoped any undercover CIA agents would blend in with the crowd. While she waited, she translated bits and pieces of conversation she overheard in Spanish and listened in on nearby tourists. Several conversations centered on the nearby Mayan ruins and things planned for the day. A few acerbic comments about husbands and boyfriends brought a slight curve to her lips.

Taking her turn at the window with the immigration official, Reese gave him the fake passport the Agency had made for her and waited as he examined it. When asked, she said she had nothing to declare. Then he asked about her plans. She told him that she would be touring the ruins and markets in Guatemala with her group. He stamped her passport and waived her on toward the area where people were waiting for luggage to be unloaded, checked by immigration and returned.

Barkley stepped up to the window. Using the rest room excuse, Reese slipped away, promising to meet him in the luggage area. Then she followed the signs down to the other end of the large room and around a corner, hoping there would be a working phone she could use to call Flaherty before Barkley caught up with her.

Finding the phones in the alcove between the rest rooms for men and women, she bit her lip. The one pay phone was broken and the other phone required a card. She lifted the receiver to make sure there was a dial tone. The expected buzz filled her ear. At the most, she figured that she had three minutes to call Flaherty and give him the information. With an eye on her watch, she lifted the receiver and put her credit card in the card slot, hoping it would work. She knew that some of the phones in Mexico only accepted the prepaid Ladatel card, but here, she had no idea. When the operator came on the line in Spanish, Reese gave her Flaherty's office number.

The familiar sound of Flaherty's voice came on the other end. "Reese, we've been trying to contact you. I—"

"I don't have much time," she interrupted. "I'm calling from a pay phone at the Aurora International Airport in Guatemala City. We're waiting for the team to clear immigration. The lab is in Guatemala. Barkley's got a man here on the ground, but something's gone wrong—he hasn't called in."

"I've already got a team in-country, Reese. They've been checking out the two sites using your information and doing surveillance. Something's not adding up," Flaherty told her. "Put the new intel you've collected on your recorder into an envelope, mark it for Cortez Andara and leave it at the front desk at any of the downtown hotels. It'll go to the embassy and be processed by our team."

Reese checked the entrance to the hall. Her time was nearly up. "Okay. I've got to go."

Stomach bubbling, Reese hung up the phone and rushed for the entrance to the hall. She nearly bumped into Barkley. "Sorry I took so long, but I had to wait," she explained.

Barkley checked the alcove, his gaze lingering on the phone and the door to the ladies room.

Just then, the rest room door opened and three women came out with a small child in tow. Reese could almost see him dismiss his suspicious thoughts.

"You gonna be okay?" he asked, managing to sound concerned.

"I'm fine."

"Then let's go. The rest of the team is nearly done with immigration."

She went back to the luggage area with Barkley and sat there with the team. After about ten minutes, the immigration official came and called Barkley by name. Then he took the group and their luggage to a separate area where their luggage was to be searched. The men talked briefly, and the official took a cursory look into one of the carry-on bags. After Barkley gave him an envelope, they were cleared.

Reese said nothing. Hidden in the team's luggage were weapons and guns that should have caused serious problems for them. She'd read that corruption was widespread in Guatemala.

"There's nothing money can't buy," Barkley said, chuckling as they left the terminal with their bags intact.

Outside, they climbed aboard a shuttle bus to the hotel. "Rest and get something to eat," Barkley advised. "You're going to be jet-lagged, and I need all of you ready for anything. It's already evening and I know you can take care of yourselves, but don't leave the hotel after dark unless you're ready to rumble with a tough crowd. Stick together and don't use the telephones. I don't want anyone to know we're here. I'll be checking on the local arrangements. We're on for late tonight, so be prepared."

As the others grabbed their bags and headed

for the check-in counter and the rooms Barkley
had reserved, Reese and Bodega lingered.

"Are you sure you don't want any help with the
arrangements?" Reese asked.

"I can handle it alone," Barkley assured her.

Taking their bags, Reese and Bodega followed
the others to check in.

Once she made it to her room, Reese discovered that she was tired and had the beginnings of
a tension headache. Still, if she hadn't already
seen Barkley take off in a taxi, she'd have followed him with her last bit of strength.

She walked around her room, checking everywhere to make sure it was secure and that she really was alone. Then she opened the drapes and
looked out to see the dark triangular shapes of
mountains rising in the distance to surround the
city.

Closing the drapes against the sunlight, she
drew back the bedcover and lay down for several
minutes to make the world stop moving. But with
discipline borne of experience, she awakened
after an hour and freshened up.

Checking her watch, she decided to check in
again with Flaherty and tell him where she was.
The phone on the dresser across the room wasn't
even a consideration. Any calls from the room

were likely to show up on her room charges for Barkley to see.

It was still light outside when she left her room to explore the hotel. Getting the lay of the land and trying to spot some of her team members, she strolled through the areas near the conference rooms, fitness center, restaurants and gift-shop areas. It was like any of a hundred hotels she'd been in, except for the mix of tourists filling the hotel and speaking several languages, predominantly Spanish.

It was easy enough to spot hotel security among the people milling about. Reese appreciated the hotel's effort to ensure the safety of its guests. Gualemala was still considered a dangerous place to travel.

She took her envelope to the front desk and left it for Cortez Andora. With that out of the way, she hurried back toward the gift-shop area where cellular phones were rented. She'd seen no pay phones on her tour.

Talking to the clerk, she realized that phone rental at the hotel was a guest service only and required a room number. She didn't want Barkley seeing that on the bill. She compared the risk of being exposed or not being able to contact Flaherty to that of heading out alone to a shop across the street. *No contest.* Sunlight still streamed in from the windows and she'd already gotten her gun from the luggage. Besides, she could take care of herself.

Reese pushed open the glass front door and stepped outside. A pleasant breeze played with her hair. People passed her on the walkway, some watching her with interest, others going about their business.

By the time she reached the corner, a group of people were waiting for traffic to clear. There was no traffic light, so the cars whizzed by. Standing with the others, she kept her elbows slightly extended to command her space, conscious of the people around her.

As she started across the street, a man who looked native turned and spoke in urgent Spanish. He offered a special tour of all the ruins at a good price. Despite the smile and harmless talk, menace lurked in his dark eyes.

"Not interested," she snapped in Spanish. This had to be some kind of trick. She kept moving.

The man followed closely, talking fast.

Instead of listening to him, she followed her instincts and whirled around to confront the man's partner. He held a knife against her waist pouch. With a quick snap of her wrist she knocked the weapon from his hands. Then she socked him in the jaw with her fist.

"Stay away from me!" she ordered.

Some in the crowd turned to watch the altercation, but no one stopped to help.

Walking backward for a few paces she kept a wary gaze on the man picking up the knife and on his partner who appeared to be torn between following her and choosing another tourist to rob. She continued across the street. Going up the block, she headed for the store with the cellular phone sign. When she glanced back, the men had disappeared among the other pedestrians.

She checked around for her team members and, spotting none, casually stepped into the store.

Later, with a small phone hidden in her pants pocket and a big block of minutes, she scanned the people on the street from the shelter of the store. Easing out into the crowd, she stopped at a convenience store and purchased bottled water and pasteurized fruit juice.

Lifting the grocery bag from the counter, she looked up to find Bodega in the entrance, looking relieved.

He couldn't have been there long. She'd checked the inside of the store and had been checking the entrance regularly.

"Is Barkley looking for me?" she asked.

His eyes darkened. "*I* am the one looking for you, *querida*. This is a dangerous place and it will be dark soon."

She nodded. "I've already had my excitement for the day. Two men tried to rob me at knifepoint while I was crossing the street."

Bodega took the bag. "We're safer in groups of two."

"I'll remember that." Reese followed him outside and back toward the hotel.

As they crossed the street, Barkley was climbing out of an olive-colored SUV.

"Who's that?" Reese asked, trying to get a make on the thick-looking native in the driver's seat.

"Most likely José Culpatan, local mafia wannabe," Bodega muttered. "He was at the top of the list Barkley discussed with me. You know that Barkley sent Carlos down here to sniff around and get a fix on where the lab might be. Then he was to line up some of the locals to help."

Reese memorized the name and the man's features. She couldn't see the faces of the two men in the back. "Carlos is dead," she murmured.

"I'd bet on that," Bodega said as they reached the other side of the street and turned toward the hotel.

The SUV drove off as Reese and Bodega got to the hotel entrance. Barkley was waiting for them, his eyes dropping to the bag of groceries and then returning to Reese.

"No juice or water in the hotel?"

"Nothing I wanted to drink," she replied calmly. She was betting that he wouldn't search everyone in the morning. "Any sign of Carlos?" she asked as they all walked into the hotel.

"He's dead," Barkley said. "I just want to know who did it and why. I hope he didn't tip off the target. José says that Carlos and three of his men never came back from a scouting trip. Afterward, José went through the area with reinforcements and found nothing unusual. They'll return in the morning to help us find the lab."

Bodega shot Barkley a quick look. "You've got information Carlos didn't have," he guessed.

Barkley grinned. "I was hoping he could verify it. Always save your hold card for the final round."

Reese took time to freshen up and change before she headed down for dinner. Barkley wanted the team to meet in the hotel restaurant for their last meal before the mission. With the television going, Reese put in a quick call to Flaherty.

"Be careful at the lab," Flaherty told her. "Our team has already checked all the Viper possibilities here and in Honduras. None matches the information Barkley had. We're checking a long-shot tip about the mountains and then withdrawing the team from Guatemala. Did you get more intel?"

"Just that José Culpatan is the local working with Barkley."

"He was at the top of our list of prospects," Flaherty said. "I've also arranged for one of the agents attached to the embassy to get a fake virus sample for you to give to Barkley. You'll have it before you leave tonight."

Shutting off the phone, Reese hurried down to dinner, her mind puzzling over the fact that the lab they would be taking tonight did not match the intelligence information Barkley was using. Was he deliberately leading them down the wrong path?

Chapter 11

Reese checked the clock. It was time to get ready for the night mission.

She still felt full from dinner. After the meal, she had excused herself from the table and checked in with the hotel front desk to see if anything had been left for her. The attendant had handed her a box of tampons. The CIA was getting clever, she'd mused. Once inside her room, she discovered inside the box a metal canister with an *X* engraved on the bottom.

She'd spent the past couple of hours going over her plan. There could be no mistakes, or she was a goner.

She donned black coveralls and boots, and went down to the lobby early with her equipment bag in one hand and the safety suit in a pack strapped to her back. Barkley was already there, a bundle of nervous energy. Bodega arrived shortly after.

"I've got a bad feeling about tonight," Barkley said, rolling his shoulders. "There was a fire at the other lab early this morning. I've gotten information from Jose, but I don't trust him. We could be walking into a trap."

"That's always a risk," Reese said.

"We'll stay on our toes," Bodega added.

With the team assembled, they left the hotel in a couple of SUVs using the route they'd planned back at the facility. People were jamming the streets of Zona Rosa, where the hotel was located. Most seemed to be having a good time, but Reese had read the warnings in the hotel literature about taking to the streets at night. She'd already had a problem in broad daylight.

The group parked in a rural-looking area close to the laboratory site and walked a short distance on a dirt path using trees and brush for cover. They found the rectangular building behind a barbed wire fence. Overhead cameras scanned the yard, and several armed guards patrolled.

Reese and Bodega used potent tranquilizer dart guns fitted with sniper scopes to take out the guards one by one. Barkley and Walters sprinted forward to cut an opening in the fence for the team within the shadows of the guard shack.

Adrenaline pumping, Reese stepped through the fence opening and went to work on the security cameras. In the silence of the night, broken only by the occasional footfall or whispered comment from a team member, she cut the all-important wires. Within seconds, it was done. The cameras stopped spinning and the displays within the shack went dark.

Now the real work began.

They waited as Bodega pulled a card from his wallet and a rectangular-shaped device from his bag. With his device positioned beneath the entry device, he slipped the card into the slot. The entry door clicked open.

Quickly replacing his tools, Bodega went first, the dart gun in one hand and the Glock pistol in the other.

He fired once, just as Reese followed him into the building.

Rounding the door, she saw a man in a white lab jacket lying on the floor. Bodega had used the more silent dart gun instead of the Glock.

Reese's gaze swept the network of halls in front of her but she recognized nothing. Except for the outside barriers to entry, all the information they had was wrong.

Barkley expressed the same thought out loud and suggested they split up to cover the lab fast and keep their radios open.

Walters drew the pack with the suit off his back. "What about the suits?"

"You shouldn't need them until we enter an actual biosafety lab," Rogers said.

By silent agreement, the group separated into teams of two. Somehow, Reese ended up with Barkley. They took the corridor to the left and followed it, methodically checking the rooms. Paraphernalia, materials and equipment used in the manufacture and packaging of drugs filled most of them. They also located a small inventory of packaged goods, but nothing close to a biosafety lab where a scientist could work in relative safety on viruses.

The last door in the corridor had a computerized lock. Using a wireless device that could access the computerized system for several seconds to reveal the right code, Reese was able to open the door. Inside, a series of interconnecting rooms with sealed doors stretched ahead.

The lock clicked behind them suddenly, and a hissing noise started above their heads and grew louder. Reese looked up and caught her breath. A white gas was wafting out of the vent near the ceiling. Pointing to it, she held her breath and pushed at the lever on the door. It was locked. They'd walked into a trap!

Reese forced down panic. She reminded herself that she could hold her breath for several minutes. Still, she felt a dull pain in her chest. Her eyes watered. If she took time to put on her suit, she wouldn't be able to work the keyboard on the wireless device needed to open the door.

Beside her, Barkley was getting his suit from the pack and putting it on. Her fingers fumbled with the computerized device as she tried to access the network and open the door. The system didn't respond to the method she'd used. The device slipped from her fingers.

Reese dropped to the floor, steadying herself with a knee on the floor and a hand on the wall. The air was clearer near the floor. A bead of moisture dripped down her nose. To her right, Barkley had most of his safety suit on. She could hear him breathing noisily through the face mask.

Her fingers flew over the tiny keys on the touchpad of the device as she tried another pathway and command to the system. When nothing happened, she started reaching for the pack on her back, worried whether she had enough breath left to get the suit on. She got the pack off and was sliding back the zipper when the lock on the door clicked.

Relief flooded her system as she pushed to her feet on shaky knees and pressed the lever on the door. It opened.

She nearly fell into the corridor, gasping for breath. As fresh air rushed into her burning lungs, she stood on shaky legs and held onto the wall.

Moving a bit slowly inside the safety suit, Barkley followed her out of the room. Releasing the seals, he lifted the vinyl helmet from his head. "That was close. I thought we'd bought it."

Still gulping air, Reese straightened. "Me, too." Scanning the corridor, she guessed that the building held other booby traps and surprises for the team. The smart thing to do was leave.

Bodega's edgy voice sounded on their intercoms. "We've got to get out of here now. I've just discovered some sort of bomb on the wall in one of the rooms. Judging by the timer, we've got two minutes to get out of here. Let's go. Everybody head for the exit!"

Reese's legs were still a bit watery and her

chest hurt from the ordeal, but she knew she could sprint the distance to the front gate in record time. After all, she ran all the time. Planting her feet, she prepared to dash for the exit.

Barkley called out to her. "Wait a minute. I need help. I can't run in this thing. Help me get out of this."

You didn't stop to help me when the room was filling up with gas. You weren't concerned about anyone but yourself. She didn't voice the thoughts, but she wanted to strangle him. Reese was not one to leave anyone to die, but delaying her escape to help Barkley was one of the hardest things she'd ever done. All things considered, the idea of Barkley dying from a bomb seemed like divine justice.

Conscious of the time slipping away, she went back and helped him out of the thick vinyl suit, which he quickly stuffed into his bag. Then she flew toward the exit and made her way to the fenced yard.

Outside, the other team members were sprinting for the safety of the area outside the gate. Reese followed with Barkley close behind. She didn't stop until she was several feet from the fence.

"Do we have everyone?" Morrison asked,

glancing around anxiously. He clapped Rogers on the shoulder.

Seeing Bodega already in the group, Reese was starting to count heads, when the thunderous sound of an explosion drew her attention back to the rectangular building. Part of the roof shot up in the air in a colorful display of red and orange flames laced with thick black smoke.

Reese stared at the violent inferno consuming the building. She had almost died twice tonight. Where was the thrill she used to get escaping from near-death situations?

"Time to go," Barkley muttered. "We don't want to be here when the police decide to investigate."

They hurried back to the vehicles at a brisk pace.

Barkley sat silent and morose for the first couple of miles of the trip back to the hotel. Then he began to curse out loud. They'd been led into a trap and someone was going to pay. He was going to get some answers from Jose Culpatan.

They left the crowded, historical streets of Guatemala City's Zone 1 and drove to a less-populated area in the hills. Reese assumed that this modest wooden structure, painted beige, was Jose Culpatan's base. Half a dozen shacks surrounded it. Joyous shouts and the sounds of laughter combined with music filtered out into the night from the structure. There was obviously a party going on.

The team got out of the SUVs and followed Barkley to the gate. The armed men patrolling the fenced yard held on to their rifles and eyed the team suspiciously.

Disliking the hostile atmosphere, Reese kept her hands near her P226. She saw that Bodega and a few of the others did the same.

Barkley hailed them in Spanish and kept talking and calling for Jose Culpatan until a man came forward to see what they wanted. Barkley's Spanish wasn't the best, but he managed to communicate. Reese listened as he told the guard that he had urgent business with Culpatan and that their leader should be disturbed immediately.

Finally Culpatan, the man she'd seen with Barkley earlier in the day, came out and invited them into the house. They ended up in a small room in the back of the house drinking the local lager beer from paper cups while Barkley and Culpatan talked. In short order Barkley explained what had happened and questioned the quality of the information that Culpatan had given Carlos.

Insulted and angry, Culpatan argued that he

had not been Carlos's only source of information. He had given Carlos the locations of the two Viper labs in the area because he did not like the way they treated his people. He had also told Carlos that one of his men had seen another group of armed men taking an older white man into the mountains with his hands tied behind his back.

"Why didn't you tell me about that?" Barkley demanded angrily in Spanish.

The furious tone of Barkley's voice caused two of Culpatan's men to arrive with guns drawn to make sure their leader was not being threatened. Culpatan waved them away and answered Barkley's question. He said that Carlos had been told of the incident and Carlos was Barkley's man. Therefore Culpatan assumed that Barkley knew. Carlos had taken to exploring the hills and mountains in the area and making records. If the information collected was not for Barkley, then who?

Barkley's expression darkened. "I'd sure as hell like to know," he grumbled. "Carlos had reams of maps and information. I looked it over but I didn't see anything unusual. I want to go to the area he was exploring when he disappeared."

Culpatan agreed to show Barkley and the team—for a price. When they'd agreed on the amount, Barkley turned to questions about the two Viper labs. This time Culpatan shrugged. He'd already informed Barkley about the morning fire at the site that was out in the countryside, and told him that both sites had had much less traffic in the past week.

Reese took in the information, wondering if the CIA team had gone into the other lab where the fire had been. If so, had the team escaped?

Reese was glad when they left Culpatan's compound. It was late when they drove back to the hotel. Most of the team members retired to their rooms, but Reese, Barkley and Bodega elected to hold a strategy session in Barkley's suite.

As Reese entered, she realized that he'd finally succeeded in getting her into his room, after all this time. So she was glad that Bodega was present, too.

Grabbing a handful of maps each, they went to work, spreading out the maps that Carlos had collected on every available surface and poring over them. Guatemala was a mountainous country. Several of the maps displayed areas in and close to the Alta Verapaz, the Sierra de las Minas, the Sierra de Santa Cruz, and the Sierra de Merendón circled with a red marker. Others featured trails that were marked in yellow. A number of maps highlighted the lab they'd managed to escape tonight and the lab where there'd been a fire.

Their excitement rose when they studied a detailed map with indications of old mines and caves. The maps were proof that Carlos had considered searching underground for the Viper lab. What better place to hide a terrorist facility?

Reese wondered how Barkley could have missed the significance of the maps, but kept her mouth shut. He'd obviously bought into the original ideas, plans and information to the exclusion of new information.

Among themselves, they made a prioritized list of the places they'd check if tomorrow's excursion netted them nothing. It was after two in the morning when they ended their meeting.

Back at her room, Reese found it hard to get to sleep. She called Flaherty and filled him on the night's activities. Flaherty told her that the CIA was ahead of Barkley in finding the lab in the mountains. They'd checked the information they had on the lab against geographic and historical information on the region. Then they'd checked their suspicions against thermal images of the area from the spy satellites and had found the lab entrance.

Stunned, she listened as Flaherty told her that a CIA team was targeting the Viper lab that very minute. By the time Barkley found the lab, the CIA would already have the African Rage virus.

Concerned about the CIA team and the deadly virus, she asked Flaherty if Nick was in-country with the team. He was.

Reese checked in again with Flaherty after her morning shower. His voice rang with regret when he told her that the CIA foray into the lab had been successful, but in the resulting exchange of gunfire, two agents had missed the pickup.

Reese forced the air from her lungs. "Tell me that Nick's not in that Viper lab," she demanded.

Flaherty's voice was strained. "I can't do that, but you know Nick. If there's a way out, he'll find it. Look for both agents and report back."

Reese couldn't eat, so she forced down tea while the team enjoyed a quick breakfast in the hotel dining room. Then they met Culpatan and some of his men for a trip to the Sierra de las Minas. It was about fifty miles from Guatemala City, but it took close to an hour and a half on the rough mountain roads.

During the ride, Reese spent the time looking at the beautiful flowers and foliage on the glorious mountain, but her thoughts were with Nick. They passed several groups on tours to the Sierra de las Minas Biological Preserve.

Reese's mind felt numb at the thought of finding Nick's body at their destination. Desperately she clung to her belief in his skill and ingenuity. Then she prayed that if he was alive, she would find him and a way to help him without blowing her cover. It was hard to stay alert and ready for anything.

At the mountain site, they hiked up to the preserve with several tourist groups and walked the most popular areas. As Culpatan had said, other than the vibrant beauty of nature and thinner air, they found nothing unusual.

Determined to cover the entire area, Barkley split the group into teams of three. Then Reese, Barkley and Bodega explored one of the isolated areas. Gradually, they made their way around to where the maps detailed a series of caves.

There was nothing in sight except for a large tent that two men had erected along the side of the mountain. They sat in folding chairs in front of it, playing cards.

Bodega checked the GPS coordinates on his hand-held tracker and glanced around again. They were close enough to be able to see the opening to the caves.

Reese followed Barkley to talk to the men about their tent, while Bodega went to fetch Culpatan and the team. Reese didn't miss the two rifles resting against the men's chairs or the slight bulge of weapons beneath their clothing. More fluent in Spanish than Barkley, Reese asked the men about the caves and the location of the opening. When the younger man made a move toward his weapon, Barkley shot both of them with a silencer.

Kneeling, Reese gathered the men's weapons and their radios. Then they pulled the tent away from a cave entrance hidden by thick green foliage. Their suspicions had been right.

Reese stepped carefully into the opening, only to discover a security-protected barrier. Examining the card reader, keyboard input and screen, she realized that it was one they'd studied at Barkley's facility. She could almost remember enough of Bodega's briefing on the system to break in.

"Let me do it," Bodega said from behind her. "I could do this one in my sleep.

As Reese moved aside she heard Culpatan and his men distancing themselves from what was about to go down. They'd shown Barkley the area where Carlos had disappeared and helped him find the lab. Now they were done. They wanted to get paid.

She saw Barkley hand over a thick envelope. Culpatan counted it, nodded and left with a smile. His men followed.

"Do you think they might come back?" Reese asked. She didn't trust Culpatan and his crew.

"No. Jose is cool. We'll do business again sometime. Besides, I sent Morrison ahead to watch the vehicles and make sure we can get out of here fast if we have to."

Nodding, Reese removed her pack. "After last night, do we dare go in without our safety suits on?"

"I wouldn't think of it," Barkley answered, drawing his pack off his shoulders too.

Bodega whispered back to them, "I've got it."

The barrier slid aside to reveal another dark chamber with dim lights overhead and a control panel with several buttons. It reminded Reese of an airlock. She pulled on the awkward suit, noting that Bodega followed her lead. They would move a bit more slowly, but they would be safe.

The rest of the team arrived and began to put on their safety suits. Bodega worked on the control panel and managed to open the door leading deeper into the cave.

The hum of a generator vibrated through the underground tunnel. An emergency light shone in the dim, air-conditioned area beyond the door. Several boxes of supplies and expensive lab equipment had been pushed into piles near the entrance. Reese wondered if they were too late. Was Viper moving its lab?

The empty main corridor beckoned. Reese felt a tingling at the back of her neck. This was too easy. There was no way the place could be empty unless the CIA came in with the local authorities and cleaned everybody out. With all she'd heard about this country, it didn't seem likely.

Nodding, Barkley went north with Morrison, taking the direct route. Reese and the young, beefy Rogers turned right at the end of the corridor, taking a less direct route.

Reese and Rogers were halfway down the next corridor when gunfire erupted in a nearby passage. Were the Viper personnel hiding and picking off Barkley's team one by one? The comm links that Barkley had given them were silent.

Plastered close to the wall, they inched along the hall, searching the area as quickly as they could. At the end, they peered into the intersection.

Empty.

Senses tingling, she paused and listened for sounds above the rapid beat of her heart and the slight hiss of the air in her suit. Gunfire sounded off and on in a nearby corridor. Having learned to trust her instincts and senses, she signaled Rogers. Then she burst across the intersection to the other side.

Waiting a couple of beats, Rogers followed. With a sudden burst of gunfire, he darted forward, only to crumple on to the floor.

Reese had to move on. Gun extended in her gloved hand, she stepped carefully, then ran lightly, ever mindful of the sound of her boots on the tiled floor. Checking the luminous dial on her watch, she saw that ten minutes had passed. She sped up.

At the next intersection she turned right again, her eyes acclimatizing to the dark passageway. She didn't dare turn on the flashlight. Just then, sound and light exploded in the air near her shoulder. Recoiling, she slammed down to the floor and knocked what little breath she had left from her lungs. Luckily, her suit remained intact.

She perceived movement as she lay there playing dead. A trickle of sweat ran down her forehead and into her eyes. The suit was hot. Using all of her senses, she peered into the darkness.

Holding herself ready, she extended her foot and tripped the person moving through the corridor. The figure tumbled to the floor. Rushing forward, Reese landed three good punches. Afraid that she might shoot Nick or the other CIA agent by mistake, she used the dart gun. Then she shone her flashlight on the face of the unconscious man.

He was Hispanic and of medium build. His coveralls were not the black and gray that Flaherty's team typically used.

Reese moved on.

In the next corridor she tripped on another body. Again she shone her flashlight on the face. She recognized Agent Raul Gonzalez. He was dead—several gunshot wounds. Reese said a quick prayer for him and his family as she turned off her flashlight.

Her heart pounded as she hurried toward area seven. She kept seeing Raul's body in her mind, his face changing to Nick's.

Up ahead, a shape blended into the darkness. Raising the dart gun, she fired. The thick sound of a body falling followed by a metallic skittering sound convinced her that she'd hit her mark.

She waited a few seconds to let the drug take effect and then used her flashlight. Another Viper gunman lay unconscious. Where was Nick?

The next passageway was clear, but Reese heard nearby gunfire. She peered around the corner. An armed man dressed in fatigues stood in front of a door, anxiously watching both ends of the passageway. His presence gave her hope. He must be guarding the lab and the virus must still be there.

Reese dropped him with her P226 when he turned to check the other end of the corridor. She saw that the card reader used to control entry to the lab had been busted.

She braced herself for a fight as she turned the lever and pulled open the door to peer into the entry. No sign of anyone. With the P226 ready, she walked into a large laboratory. The Biosafety Level 4 portion of the lab lay in front of her. Previous experience and the hours of training and instruction with Dr. Reynolds kicked in as she studied the control panel. As expected, everything was still working.

The video surveillance system seemed to be functioning. Intent on zeroing in on the specific area where the viruses were, she flicked through several video displays on the monitor. In one room, the bodies of four men in white lab coats lay in various positions on the floor, unmoving. Reese could only guess what had been done to them. The dead eyes bulged on one body lying face-up to the camera, one hand charred.

Then she saw another room with a man sitting in a corner, sweat running down his handsome face, his body shivering despite the black turtle-neck and matching slacks.

"Nick!" she gasped, her eyes glued to the display. *He's alive. Dear God, he's alive.*

Chapter 12

Dread filled Reese as she stared at him in the little room pictured on the screen. Nick was sweating and shaking; both were symptoms of the African Rage virus.

I'm really going to lose him this time. Tears burned her eyelids. She didn't know what to do. Her fists slammed against the panel. She couldn't stand to lose another person she loved. She couldn't stand to lose Nick, she just couldn't. She had to get him out of there, get him to where he could be cured. *There is no cure.* The thought repeated itself in the chaos of her mind, but she refused to give in to it.

Reese shot through the first chamber with the protective clothing and pawed through the suits until she found one that would fit Nick. Adding black chemical-resistant gloves and boots, she carried her load through the next area where a chemical shower was set up to sterilize the suits of exiting scientists. Finally, she came through to an open area at the end that had been divided into small rooms.

With the extra suit in her arms, she hurried past the automatic door into the series of small labs. In a temperature-controlled room, Reese found the pressurized cabinet containing all the viruses with which they'd been working.

On the stainless steel canister in the number six position, Reese read the Latin name for the African Rage virus. The bottom of the canister was marked with an *X*. That confirmed that the CIA had successfully retrieved the virus. Taking the CIA canister and placing it in the container on her belt, she placed the one that had been left in her hotel room in another spot.

Then she checked the waterproof watch she wore on the outside of her suit—and thought her heart would stop. According to their plan, she had twelve minutes left. Within that time, she had to get the suit to Nick and give him a chance to get a CIA extraction. There was still the possibility of finding a cure. It was his only chance.

In frantic haste, she looked through the double-paned glass on the door of each room. Nick's was the last and the door was locked. Dropping the suit, she picked the lock with a tool from her belt. Then she entered the room to approach her husband.

His jaw was tight, determination burning in his eyes. She couldn't help noticing that his thick black hair was tightly curled and matted with sweat, and he was still shivering. He leaned against the wall, arms raised to block a blow, obviously marshalling his strength for an attack. Even in his debilitated state, Nick could be hell to deal with.

Shaking her head, she extended one gloved hand, fingers splayed in the signal for him to stop. Then she pointed to the suit on the floor of the entryway.

Nick came off the wall, body tensing.

The intercom attached to the suit interfaced with the other lab suits, so she couldn't talk to him. With a deep breath, Reese stepped back in a defensive posture, hoping she wouldn't have to hurt him. Her heart hammered so loudly she could barely think. If they fought, they could both end up infected.

She drew the P226 from her waistband and pointed it at him, something she'd never thought she'd have to do. It took everything she had to hold it steady. Nick would challenge any sign of weakness.

He dropped his arms, slumped his shoulders in defeat.

Reese sighed in relief. She stared at her lover, teacher and partner and knew that she'd spent the past few months fooling herself.

Watching him, assessing his state of mind, she came closer, giving him a chance to recognize her features beneath the helmet. His eyes widened. Then she watched his wide, sensual mouth form her name. She lowered the gun.

Nick came close, his eyes penetrating her very soul as he peered into her helmet. He told her that he loved her and managed to get his arms around her beneath the air cylinder and hose.

She closed her eyes and, for several moments, something deep and true passed between them. Her body shook inside the suit. Her heart ached with a searing pain.

In a sudden gesture that telegraphed defeat, he dropped his arms and backed away. *Leave me.*

And this time she knew he was right.

She choked on the thought. Her Nick, handsome and heroic with a big heart, considered himself a dead man. She didn't need to check her watch to know that they were running out of time. Turning away from him, she retrieved the suit from the doorway and thrust it in his hands. When he shook his head, she pounded his shoulder with her fist and pointed to her watch.

With a look of resignation, Nick climbed into the suit.

Reese hooked the air hose and tank to his suit and switched on his suit intercom system.

"Reese—"

The sound of his deep baritone permeated her soul, giving her hope. What happened?" she asked, needing to know.

"After we got the virus, we sent most of the team to the pickup point while we stayed to search for Ballinger and the work on the cure." Nick paused to take several deep breaths. "By the time I realized that he wasn't here, it was too late. They'd killed my partner and caught me close to the exit. I went through a short interrogation, then they locked me in this room. I think they exposed me to the virus."

"We've got to get out of here Nick," she said, attempting to keep them both on task.

"How much air do I have in this thing?" he asked, looking for the gauge.

Praying for at least a couple of hours, she located it and read from the dial. "Approximately ninety minutes."

He stepped forward, his gloved hand gripping hers as their helmets touched. "Reese, sweetheart, I love you more than anything this world can dream. I wasn't there when you needed me and I hate that you had to go through so much pain all alone. It stands between us, even now."

"No, not now," she countered, noting every detail, from the pronounced grooves on his forehead and the signs of illness and strain in his dark eyes, to the cracked skin on his full lips. "I was hurt and angry, but I— I don't want it to end like this." Her statement ended with something close to a sob.

"You're not going to lose me, because this is not the end," he promised. Nick always kept his promises, but Reese knew that this one was out of his hands.

"I'm holding you to your promise," Reese said, getting herself under control.

Nick didn't answer.

Neither of them spoke as they ran for the chemical shower. While the spray washed over their suits, she found herself praying again.

"You'll have to make the call for extraction," Nick said grimly as they hurried out of the final chamber.

They took two steps toward the lab entrance, only to halt as the door opened. Drew Walters stood in the opening in a pair of navy overalls with his gun pointed at them, his gray eyes shining with malice. Static punctuated his voice, but they could hear him.

"Isn't this a pretty picture? The closer I got to this lab, the clearer you two came in on the suit intercom. I swear Barkley's about gone crazy trying to get you on the comm link. I can't wait to hear what you'll say about your friend here."

Turning with one hand behind her back, she spoke quickly and with conviction. "Don't shoot or we'll all die. This man had been infected with the African Rage virus."

Walters smiled, the evil in it sending chills down her spine. "Human experimentation? I can appreciate that. I know Barkley will. Maybe he'll add *you* to the list of lab rats when he hears the details of your conversation." He chuckled, and then began to laugh in earnest. "You've made things easy for me."

She stilled, her expression blank as her fingers closed on the P226.

"Let me get Barkley on the comm," Walters said, lifting his free hand.

In a flash she had the pistol out and fired.

A red hole appeared in his chest, spouting a fountain of his blood. He dropped the gun and stumbled, holding his chest. "You bitch!" he grunted, then crumpled to the floor.

Nick kicked the gun away from Walters' convulsing form and picked it up with gloved hands. She'd had no choice but to eliminate Walters. She'd always known deep in her heart that her problems with Walters would end with his death. But she still felt a stab of guilt at taking another life. Even that of a lowlife like Walters.

Reese's hands shook as she retrieved the cell phone she'd bought in Guatemala City and called Flaherty. He answered immediately.

"It's Reese. I got Nick, but he's been infected. No time to talk, but he needs extraction now."

She ended the call abruptly, opened the doors to the lab and looked out. The corridors were dark since the generator had been silenced and the emergency lights were scattered. Reese plunged ahead, trying not to worry about Nick as she walked the path she had plotted at the facility to reach Barkley's position. When she made a turn, she realized that Nick had taken off.

Maybe it was better that they hadn't had a chance to say goodbye, she thought as she rounded a corner with her gun drawn. But worry for Nick consumed her, crowding her thoughts and making her heart ache. She struggled to focus on the mission. It was better that he wasn't caught with her by Barkley and the team. Now she had to get out so she could get him extracted.

Someone was hiding against the wall. Steadying the pistol, she made out the outlines of a safety suit. She reached for her flashlight.

"Reese, don't shoot." Arturo Bodega's richly accented voice echoed in her ears.

"How did you know it was me?" she asked, startled.

"Two things," he said, a smile in his voice, "Your suit and your height. And maybe a connection we both share."

After seeing Nick, the intimacy in Bodega's tone bothered her.

"I just managed to escape from a trap. Stack bought it with a head shot. You get the Rage virus?" he asked.

"Yes," she answered. "But they got Walters, Rogers took a hit, and I've been having a problem with my comm link going in and out. I was circling back to help Barkley."

She felt the weight of his gaze and was glad that he couldn't see her face. In the ensuing silence she wondered if Bodega had seen or heard her with Nick and Walters. He'd gotten much too close without her noticing. Had he been following her? Did he have an agenda of his own? She kept her hand on the gun, ready for anything.

"Try the comm again," he suggested, "If it doesn't work, I'll tell Barkley it's time to move for the exits."

Glad Bodega couldn't see what she was doing she spoke into the comm, switching it on and off to simulate an intermittent problem. "Whittaker here with Bodega. I've got the package so we're good to go."

"Excellent!" Barkley's voice boomed in her ear, punctuated with the occasional sound of gunfire. "What about Ballinger and the cure?"

"No sign of either." Reese heard Bodega echoing her words to others in the background.

Barkley continued. "We're trapped in the west corridor bordering area three. I've been trying like hell to raise you on the comm to make sure you had it before we busted out of here."

"We ran into problems." Reese launched into the story she'd given Bodega.

"It's past time for us to get the hell out of here,"

Barkley said when she finished. "See if you can't open it up for us."

"Will do. Whittaker out." She and Bodega moved on, turning at the next intersection to go north. Advancing through unfamiliar territory, Reese slowed, conscious of every sound. She and Bodega took turns taking the lead and running ahead to act as point man while the other followed.

At corridor N31, gunfire erupted around them. Separating to make themselves harder to hit, they advanced low to the ground, somewhat handicapped by the suits but ducking into doorways and checking open areas. Coordinating fire, they cleared the area clean through to corridor W29.

Reese and Bodega covered the corridor with a spray of gunfire while Barkley and Morrison made their escape, then fell in behind them as they raced for the exit.

Outside, Bodega covered the exit while they stripped off their suits. Half the group started the hike out of the preserve and back down to the vehicles while Reese covered Bodega as he rid himself of his suit.

"Fresh air," Bodega said, quickly stuffing the suit into the bag. "I hated that thing, but I did not dare take it off."

"Me neither—"

Just then, someone ran out of the exit with a gun. Before Reese could react, Bodega took him out.

Reese tensed momentarily, then, satisfied that it wasn't Nick, she hurried after Bodega.

Barkley was jubilant when they arrived back at the training facility. "Don't go anywhere or plan anything 'cause we're going to celebrate tonight!" he told them.

"A bath and my bed are on the top of my list," Reese said, aware for the first time of the deep weariness settling over her.

"I second that."

Bodega's voice was like a caress against her skin. Reese was careful not to look at him. That would be encouraging him and waving a red flag in front of Barkley.

"Oh, your things have been moved back to your old quarters," Barkley announced as they walked away. "After a few days' rest, you'll be back teaching the recruits. We'll talk about the proceeds of this project at the party tonight."

After acknowledging his statement, they headed for their quarters. Uncharacteristically silent, Bodega kept pace with Reese. Not ready to deal with anything beyond getting the software encryption codes and bringing Barkley in, she didn't speak either.

"Maybe we can talk later," Bodega said, as she turned off to enter the floor for the women's quarters.

"I'd like that." She fit her key into the lock, turned it and opened the door. "See you later."

"Until later..."

Bodega's voice curled around the words, offering a comfort she knew she could not accept.

Stepping through the doorway, she continued down the hall to her room. The muscles in her legs throbbed from crouching low for long periods of time and her arm was sore from holding the gun for most of the time she'd been in the lab. She could almost see a dark cloud hanging over her head, filled with fear and worry for Nick.

Inside, she locked the door and jammed a chair beneath it. Her things from the other side of the facility were packed in neat cardboard boxes that had been placed on the desk. The clothing she'd left in the room prior to working the project was still in the drawers and closets.

Grabbing a couple of towels and a change of clothes, she went into the bathroom and filled the bathtub with hot water. Despite a perm, her hair was wild and bushy from the moist mountain air in Guatemala. She toyed with the idea of simply wrapping it in a towel while she bathed and curling it into submission afterward, but it was dirty too.

Reese climbed into the tub and scooted down deep in the hot, soothing liquid. Gradually, some of the pain and tension in her body eased, seeping into the water. She helped the process along with a technique she'd learned long ago. In her mind's eye, the dark cloud lightened, some of its weight escaping in a rain that was not unlike tears.

She let out a deep sigh and opened her eyes, her face wet with steam and tears. Nick had less than three days for a miracle and she had to get the code before she could even think of helping him. Besides, she'd given Barkley the fake virus and wasn't sure how soon it would take Dr. Reynolds to figure out it wasn't the real thing.

On the sides of the tub her hands formed hard fists. She had to act tonight. There was no other choice.

While the water in the tub ran out slowly, she climbed into bed and thought about her first mission with Nick.

Their assignment was to use their contact to

get into a party being held at the offices of an Italian power broker and obtain proof that he was secretly working with a terrorist group. Handsome, sexy and talented, Nick had fascinated her and they were hot for each other, but she worried that the flame would go out and he would move on, never looking back. He wasn't the type to declare his love to any woman and settle down.

Nick usually worked with Agent Raven Ramone, but Reese had just lost another partner and Flaherty was trying out a hunch that she and Nick would work well together.

As soon as they got into the unmarked car to head to the party, Nick pulled her into his arms and gave her a deep, intoxicating kiss that left her head spinning. She leaned back against the seat, breathing hard, her body aching for more.

"I liked that, but it's no way to start the assignment," she admonished him.

"It is when you're nervous." He took her hands in both of his and massaged them. "This isn't a test, it's for real. We both have a job to do. Relax and just do your part. Don't worry about me. I can take care of myself a lot better than you can. If I'm not back at the meeting place by ten-thirty sharp, and you haven't heard from me, take off."

Reese spent half the party dancing with several very drunk men before she saw her chance to get into her target's office alone. It took her less than five minutes to find the file she was looking for in a stack on the desk and photograph it.

But the two guards who had left their post in front of the office returned—and she was stuck. She decided to pop out and tell them she'd wanted to give their boss a special present in his office, but that she was tired of waiting.

"Stay here," they ordered as she bolted for the exit—only to run straight into another guard. With a running start, she knocked the guy out with a quick wellplaced front kick to the face with her two-inch rhinestone-studded heels. Then she hurried down the hall.

Nick was waiting for her outside the exit with a cocky expression on his face and deep admiration in his eyes. "Good job," he said. "You're a lethal beauty. I saw how you handled Romeo and those guards. I love a lady who can hold her own."

"I'll have to remember that," she said as they both darted for the car.

They'd just finished their debriefing at CIA Headquarters and were headed for their cars to go home when Nick made his final strategic move for the night.

"I want you," he said, his expression serious. "It's all I've been thinking about for the past four hours." He caressed her face while her closer. He planted a soft kiss on her lips and said, "Baby, you rock. Spend the night with me? Say yes."

Reese remembered the heat of his body tingling along the surface of her skin. "Yes. I can't wait to feel you all over." Leaning forward, she opened her mouth and let her tongue dance and slide against his. Warm tendrils of sensation spread through her from everywhere they touched, and dipped low to curl in her stomach. She felt Nick's heart pounding.

She broke the kiss, her own heart beating like a drum.

"There'll be a picture of us like this on my desk in the morning," he mused, referring to the surveillance cameras.

"I don't care," she told him, opening the door with the remote. "I wanted that kiss."

"You got it. And me too." He looked like he wanted to devour her. "My place in ten minutes?"

"Five," she answered, fitting her key into the ignition. Nick was running to his car as she took off.

Minutes later, as soon as they were inside his

apartment, they were all over each other, touching, licking, kissing and delving into layers of clothing.

"Nick," she gasped when his hot mouth closed on the aching nipple of one breast and he slid his hand into her black lace panties to caress her intimately. Sizzling currents of sensation fed the storm within her as she squirmed against Nick. When she collapsed against him, he picked her up and carried her into the bedroom.

Reese remembered loving every minute as she stripped Nick of the rest of his clothes. Long and lean-muscled, he had rock-hard abs, a firm, well-shaped butt, wide shoulders and sculptured biceps. Fifteen minutes later she was on her back crying out in ecstasy while he thrust into her with a wild, explosive rhythm. Rocking up against Nick, she felt her insides melt as they reached a pinnacle and floated back to earth.

Turning over now, Reese reached out to touch Nick's warmth, but closed on a cold pillow. She opened her eyes. She was alone. Sitting up, she drew her knees to her chest, the fingers of one hand knifing through her damp hair. She'd been dreaming about Nick again. What was she going to do when there was nothing left but the dream?

A firm series of knocks sounded on her door,

startling her. "Who is it?" she called, pulling on her robe and retrieving her pistol from beneath her pillow.

No one answered, but the rapping continued.

Slipping the pistol into the pocket of her robe, she peered through the peephole. What the hell? No men were allowed on the ladies' floor. *If you own the place you can break your own rules....*

Straightening, she drew the edges of her bathrobe tighter and removed the chair from beneath the doorknob. The locks clicked as she opened the door. "Yes?"

Barkley took in the wild hair around her face, the bathrobe and her bare feet. A smile spread across his face. "Get enough sleep?"

"Not quite." Still sluggish, she leaned against the door frame, waiting for him to get to the point.

"I could come in, give you a massage and help you sleep," he offered, his voice oozing charm.

"Oh, I think I can manage," she countered in a pleasant voice.

He pressed his point. "Better yet, you could come to my quarters and we could work out the chemistry that's been simmering between us, and start our own explosion."

"Is that why you came over here?" She allowed a little disappointment to leak into her voice.

"No, but seeing you stand here like that sure brings it to mind. You got something exclusive going with Bodega or is there just something about me you don't like?"

There was *a lot* about him that she didn't like—at the top of list, his part in her brother's death and his willingness to sell out his country for money. Still, there was something that she did like and had been struggling with. Was it his boyish charm, or the fact he so obviously had a thing for her?

Reese smiled and spoke without hesitation. "I don't have anything going with Arturo but friendship. Are you interested in that?"

"I'm interested in *you*." He came so close that their faces almost touched. One hand reached out to caress her cheek, his green eyes assessing her reaction.

"Then take it real slow," she said, willing herself not to stiffen beneath his touch.

Dropping her hand, he took a half step back. "I actually came to give you a personal invite to tonight's celebration. I'm having steak and lobster brought in for the team, and the booze will be free for everyone."

"Sounds good." She shifted away from the door frame. "What about our money?"

"It'll be in your hands in a couple of days."

She smiled. "Good. What time is dinner?"

"At six in my private dining room. There're no limits on how long the party goes on."

"I'll be there," she said with a nod.

The charm-filled smile returned. "Fine. See you there...and wear something nice."

She lifted one brow and gave him a quelling look.

"Or not," he added, grinning. Then he turned and walked back toward the heavy barrier door to the men's facility.

The muscles in her neck and shoulders were tight as she shut and locked the door and replaced the chair. She didn't have much time. Tonight was the night to get into Barkley's quarters, and the disk and get out of the training facility—with or without Barkley.

She dressed in a form-fitting black top with slim black pants that accentuated her curves, added lipstick, and slipped on her black boots. With a curling iron she tamed the wild mess of her hair into a mass of curls.

Reese tossed a jacket over one arm in case she got cold and made her way to the mess building with twenty minutes to spare. It was still bright and pleasant outside, the orange-gold globe of the sun just starting to dip beyond the greenery-fringed horizon in a glorious display of nature. She stopped to enjoy the view. Staring at it, she felt an overwhelming sense of hope that everything she planned to do tonight would work out and she'd be at Nick's side tomorrow.

Alone in Barkley's private dining room, Bodega already sat in a padded leather armchair dressed in a stone-colored linen jacket with matching pants and a deep-blue sport shirt. His gaze covered her like a warm caress. "Reese, you light the room with your presence."

Enjoying his warmth and sincerity, she thanked him. She liked his outfit too, and the way it enhanced his muscular body and contrasted with his golden skin, but decided not to get into the compliment game. She placed her jacket on the back of the chair next to him and sat down.

"I had a personal wake-up call from Barkley."

"So did I," he replied in a mellow voice. "He is still very much excited about us completing the project successfully."

"I'm excited too." She signaled to the waitress and ordered a shot of tequila. They sat in companionable silence until the waitress brought her drink. "To success," she declared then, raising her glass.

"And long may it continue," he added with a chuckle. They drank from their glasses. He lowered his voice. "Have you thought of a time and place to talk?"

"No," she answered honestly.

He grabbed the fingers of her free hand, held them a moment, then released them.

She toyed with the stem of her glass. "I told Barkley about my friendship and affection for you."

Eyes of liquid night studied her closely. "There is so much more in what I feel for you, *querida*."

Reese swallowed hard. Alcohol really did release the inhibitions, and that could be a dangerous thing. His words danced along the surface of her skin. Her pulse sped up. She could actually imagine herself making love with Arturo Bodega and knew it would be intense and exciting.

But it was a fantasy they could never fulfill. Her heart was with Nick. Besides, with her plans for the evening, the opportunity would never arrive. Still, she couldn't bring herself to make him think she didn't care at all.

She found her voice. "Arturo, denying you would be difficult, but we need to discuss this in the privacy it deserves."

"Of course, *querida*." His voice was intimate and apologetic. Then he fell silent.

Morrison arrived, his black hair slicked back and his blue eyes glowing. Dressed in a white shirt and tan slacks, he flashed them a smile. "I'm early?" he asked, glancing around the room.

Behind him, the waitress set a platter filled with shrimp, egg rolls and cocktail sausages on the table. "Dinner will be served in about five minutes," she said. "Would you like a drink?"

Morrison's lips curved upward. "Why yes, I would. Bring me a bottle of Old Grand-Dad." While the waitress bustled off to get his drink, Morrison took the chair on the other side of Reese. "You'all hear the news about Rogers?"

She nodded. "I heard that his surgery went well and he'll be back in a couple of days."

"Yeah, and I'm glad to hear it. He's a smart kid." Morrison pulled a cigar from an inside pocket, unwrapped it and put it in his mouth. He was searching for his lighter when Barkley walked into the room.

Barkley wore a dark green casual suit with a gold sheen. It brought out the green of his eyes and the highlights in his blond hair. "Hello, everybody. I hope you're ready to eat, drink and celebrate!"

Reese swallowed and pasted on a smile. She couldn't celebrate until Barkley and the disk were in the hands of the government and she knew that Nick would be okay.

They ate dinner in the private dining room, feasting on steak and lobster tail. Afterward, Barkley pulled out playing cards and they all joined in on several games of poker.

Finally folding her hand of cards, Reese effected an elaborate yawn, stood and pretended to sway. "I'm turning in. I'm tired."

"So soon? It's only nine o'clock." Barkley looked up from his cards. There was a nice stack of bills and change in front of him. "If you'll wait a few minutes, I'll walk you back to your quarters."

"So you're that sure of your hand?" Morrison asked, peering down at his own.

Barkley didn't answer. His attention was on her.

Bodega held his cards without comment. He nodded a good-night to Reese.

Something in his confident expression told her that he was the one with the winning hand. All night he'd been quietly winning the poker games that counted.

She turned to Barkley and said, "Thanks for the offer, but I can take care of myself."

"I'll say," Morrison's laughter reminded her of a hyena's. He was drunk.

Apparently not willing to make a scene in front of the guys, Barkley gave in, turning back to his cards. Reese knew instinctively that he hadn't given up, just postponed the inevitable. Kevin Barkley would be making another trip to her room tonight.

She planned to make her escape before he got around to it.

Chapter 13

The cluster of streetlights outside the two-story building that housed Barkley's quarters had an ominous glow in the waning evening light. She took the wooden steps at an even pace, mentally rehearsing different versions of what she would say when she got inside. When she turned the knob and opened the heavy, steel-reinforced door, she found the entryway empty.

She peered into the wider area reception area. A lone guard sat at the old wooden desk, watching a set of monitors. There were supposed to be two of them.

The guard glanced up at her as she approached. "Ms. Whittaker."

She strolled to the desk and traced a finger along the edge. "I'm here for Mr. Barkley."

"You're welcome to wait here with me, ma'am." He indicated a padded leather chair next to his.

"You mean I don't have the option of going upstairs to get cozy while I wait?"

"No, ma'am, it's the rules since that other instructor got killed when someone busted into Barkley's room."

He was talking about Lana. "Okay, I'll join you," she told him, leaning against the counter. "You got anything to drink? And am I going to have to get up when your partner comes back?"

"I don't drink while I'm working," he began as he opened a drawer and rummaged through it, "but my partner keeps some of those little bottles of liquor, you know, for emergencies." He came up with a handful of miniature bottles that included rum, gin and vodka.

Reese accepted rum. "Thanks."

"You're welcome, ma'am, and you won't have to get up. I'm the only one on duty tonight."

"That makes me feel better," she said honestly, now that she only had to deal with the guard in front of her. "If you won't drink with me, at least let me refresh your coffee."

He agreed reluctantly. "Okay, but I take it black, no cream or sugar."

Reese took his cup over to the little stand alongside the opposite wall. In the bottom of the cup she placed a small tablet, then she filled it to the top with coffee.

"Did Barkley give you a time to meet him here?" he asked, accepting the cup and thanking her.

"No, but I have a standing invitation." She settled into the seat.

"I could page him for you," he offered, sipping the hot liquid.

"Let's give him a few minutes," she suggested, opening the bottle. She lifted it, tapping the little bottle against the guard's cup. "To a job well done."

"Here, here." He took a big gulp of coffee, then set the cup down. "Wow, that's some strong coffee."

"Are you okay?" Reese asked in feigned concern.

"Nah, wait a minute..." Then he collapsed onto the desk.

Closing the bottle and dropping it into her

pocket, she disabled the guard station displays of the upstairs rooms. Then she raced up the stairs to the room she'd already identified as Barkley's.

Outside the largest suite, she saw that Barkley had changed the locks and installed an electronic key sensor. In the middle of retrieving her tools to work on the lock, a new idea occurred to her.

She ran back downstairs to rifle through the guard's clothing. In an inside pocket she found a set of electronic keys. Back upstairs she tried each one, until the lock hummed and she got a green light. Opening the door carefully, she used her flashlight to check for sensors and booby traps. There were none.

She closed the door carefully and turned on the lights, scanning the room. The large sleigh bed managed to look massive yet stylish. There was a gray abstract quilt covering it. She crossed the plush carpet to check the wall near the desk.

Racking her brain, she tried to remember Larry's exact words about the location of the sliding wall mechanism. As she knocked and patted the wall, she listened for a hollow sound, trying to rein in her frustration at not finding it right away. *If Larry found it...*

Her fingers slid over a rise and sank into indentations that failed to register with her eyes. She rubbed, patted, pushed and prodded for what seemed an eternity. Finally she heard a *click,* and a small piece of the wall rotated out. She pressed the black button on the bottom, her spirits soaring when a section of the wall slid back to reveal a small office.

She used her flashlight to check for traps. The little room was dark, but light filled it from behind her when she moved to enter. A desk with a computer, a media center and a safe packed the space. Reese zeroed in on the safe, noting the type. It was a Fort Knox Double Gold and would take a while.

Ten minutes later she'd done it. *Hot damn!* Wiping the sweat off her brow with the crook of her arm, Reese was ready to do a celebration dance.

The safe's knob turned easily as she used it to pull open the door. Gritting her teeth, she cursed at the sight of another lock system. She didn't have time for this! The small, modular unit required Barkley's thumb and index fingers.

Pushing herself, she found the small spray bottle of quick-dry fixative in her bag and scanned the room for places to get Barkley's fingerprints. The bottle of Jack Daniel's and the empty glass on the nightstand were her first choices. Slipping on a pair of surgical gloves, she sprayed them both, blowing on them to speed up the process. The clearest prints were on the glass. Peeling the clear, dry, rubbery substance from the glass, she removed her gloves and applied the forms to her fingertips. She then pressed them against the lock's sensor and held her breath. If this trick didn't work, she suspected, the alarm system would go off.

She heard a *click* and the inner door sprang open.

With her flashlight she illuminated the items inside. She saw a gorgeous diamond ring, necklace and earrings in a jeweler's case, four-foot-high stacks of hundred-dollar bills, a bunch of files, and, at the very back, a rectangular blue-and-black case. *Bingo!* She opened the case and saw the code disk programmed by Dr. Conover.

Engraved on the small label she found what she was looking for: Property of the United States Government, Dr. Jess Conover, Eyes of the Beholder Project. Now she could make sure that Barkley paid for his part in her brother's death, and get back to Nick and do everything possible to make sure that he lived.

Reese froze at the sound of someone grabbing the doorknob outside the room. She had her SIG

P226 in her hand and ready when she heard a key in the electronic lock. The door opened slowly.

She saw Barkley and the gun in his hand before he saw her. Confident of her accuracy and aiming for his kneecap, she fired.

With a pain-filled yelp he went down, clutching his leg and dropping the gun. She trained the gun on him, stepping forward to kick his gun out of his reach.

"Reese!" His voice held a note of hurt surprise.

She slipped the disk into a pouch attached to her belt, quashing the guilt that raced through her. This dirty bastard had caused the death of so many people. He didn't deserve pity, sympathy, or even the truth.

"Get in the office," she ordered in a cold voice she'd never used with him.

Using his hands, butt and bent good leg, he moved forward, as if he would obey. But Reese saw his hand snake out toward the gun he'd dropped. She fired again, this time putting a hole through his palm.

Crying out, he hunched forward, cradling his hand.

"I don't have all day," she said. Gesturing with the gun, she let him know that firing another bullet would be no problem.

He scooted in awkwardly on his butt and the good hand and leg, the wet red area on his pant legs growing wider by the second. Blood from his hand dripped down his arm.

Her eyes narrowed as he made it through the doorway. His body was tensing. Barkley was up to something.

Suddenly he fell toward her, his hand hidden by the bulk of his body. "Help me," he groaned.

She stepped a little closer, suddenly certain he'd pulled a knife. He was hurt, yeah, but Barkley was a tough bastard. As she gave his shoulder a push with her free hand, his hidden hand came up with a blade.

She kicked it out of his hand and punched him in the face with her left fist. "You can thank me for not putting a hole through your head," she snapped at the sound of his painful grunt. "You know me better than to think I'd fall for that shit."

She kept her distance as she kicked the door shut. She had to get out of there. The other guard would be returning soon.

"So you were here for the code?" he asked, his green eyes zeroing in on her. "Or are you planning to take the virus too? Is Bodega in it with you?"

Not answering, she came close and put her

knee in his back and the pistol to his head. "I've got an itchy trigger finger, so don't try anything else or I'll put a bullet through that pile of crap you call a brain."

His eyes widened. "What are you? CIA? FBI? Or ATF?" When she didn't answer, he continued. "You could knock me out, take the code, the virus, and go. Unless this is personal…"

She gritted her teeth. "It *is* personal. Tell me about the embassy bombing in Rwanda."

Sweat broke out on his forehead. He was losing a lot of blood. Was he going into shock?

"I don't know anything about it."

That he would lie and think she couldn't see through it shot her temperature up. She lifted one leg and viciously kicked his wounded hand.

He cried out, his whole body shaking. Then he slumped against the wall, cradling his hand.

"I could kick your knee too," she threatened. "Make you beg me to kill you."

Barkley shivered. Then his words came out, punctuated by pain-filled sighs and groans. "The Rwandan Freedom Fighters bombed the embassy to stir things up and embarrass the government."

"That was in the newspapers." Reese pressed harder, flexing her finger on the trigger. "And?"

Squinting, he dipped his head and spoke with

reluctance. "I was part of the group that supplied the training, weapons and explosives."

"I should just kill you right now," she sputtered, anguish burning her insides like acid. "I'd do the world a favor and get some justice for all the lives you've taken."

Hunched over on the good knee, cradling his wounded hand, Barkley shook under the pressure of her verbal assault. "No, don't do it! I've got info, something worth trading my life for."

A bitter laugh burst from her lips. "What is it? I'd get so much satisfaction from seeing you dead."

He raised his head to look at her. "They're not all dead. Some of the people from the embassy are still alive."

Riley? Still alive? The hand with the gun wavered. It was too good to be true. But they had never found his body. "Where? Where are they?"

Barkley gulped air, his eyes still trained on her and the gun. "They're in Rwanda, in a Rwandan Freedom Fighter camp."

"I don't believe you," she snapped, fighting hope. "Why would they keep prisoners?"

"For a bargaining chip in case the government came after them," he answered quickly.

Her ears rang so loudly that she had to struggle to think. If Barkley was telling the truth, the CIA would want him alive for questioning. Riley's life could depend on him, which meant she had to bring him in alive. Raising the pistol in a sudden arc, she brought it crashing down on his head.

Barkley slumped forward, out cold.

Reese retrieved a couple of ties from Barkley's closet and used one to tie a tourniquet above his knee. With the other she bandaged his hand. Then she tied him up with some of his own belts.

She reached into Barkley's pocket and found his cell phone. Switching it on, she called Flaherty, told him that she'd gotten the code disk, and filled him in on the information Barkley had revealed about Rwanda.

"I'm sending in the local boys to clean the place out," Flaherty told her. "You can sit tight and we'll have a team there to pick you and Barkley up as soon as possible, or you can go to the extraction point."

"I'll go to the extraction point," she said quickly, knowing that she couldn't waste valuable time baby-sitting a trussed-up Barkley at the camp. "How's Nick?" she asked, before he could end the connection.

"He's—He's doing as well as can be expected."

"And what the hell does that mean?" She knew her tone was sharp.

"Reese, he's got the African Rage virus. We've got the best doctors we could find taking care of him. At the last briefing they told me that all of his vital organs are still functioning."

Gripping the phone hard and forcing air through her lungs, Reese signed off with Flaherty. She knew that if Nick was to have any chance of survival, she had to find the cure.

She pulled herself together, made sure Barkley was securely tied, then went back to the guard station. She was elated when she saw a supplies dolly near the huge double doors. With its wide wooden base and rubber wheels, it was big enough for Barkley's body, but also low enough to require minimum lifting.

She trekked through the hall until she found the old service elevator at the back of the building. As she rolled the dolly to Barkley's quarters she gave herself a pep talk. Soon she would have this assignment completed successfully and be free—to do everything she could for Nick and Riley.

Chapter 14

The old elevator was slow. Reese used the time to catch her breath. By the time she had made it down to the first floor she knew she was on the home stretch.

She rolled the dolly through the double doors and out to the cemented loading area. Heart hammering relentlessly, she kept one hand on the dolly and the other close to her pistol.

Her gaze darted around nervously, but she walked slowly and steadily across the parking lot, minimizing the sound made by the rubber wheels. To make things easier and take advantage of the protection of the partially enclosed loading area, she left the dolly and Barkley to get her car, which she hadn't been in since she arrived. It felt good to sit within its relative safety and protection.

On the way back in the car she caught movement in her peripheral vision. She stared out into the darkness, trying to discern shapes and forms. The night presented an impenetrable wall. She waited several minutes, then continued to the loading area for Barkley.

After popping open the trunk, she got out of the car—

"Going somewhere?"

Startled, Reese recoiled as if she'd been shot. One hand going for her P226, she turned. It was Bodega.

There was a dangerous light in his dark eyes, though his expression was calm. He'd changed the stone-colored outfit for a black shirt and pants.

"Don't draw the gun, *querida*. I'm as fast as you are, maybe faster. We don't want to shoot each other."

Was he here for Barkley? Or the disk? And why? She thought about his work with the Brazilian Special Forces and discarded the idea. If the

Brazilian Special Forces were after the disk, Flaherty would know. They were allies. Bodega had to be representing someone else.

Either way, she had to win this one.

As much as his deep, accented voice caressed her ears, her fingers itched for the gun. She had to be in control, she couldn't let him stop her. She knew she might have to hurt him.

"Walk away from this," she ordered. "You were never here."

"But I am here." He stepped closer. "And I cannot walk away, especially if you've recovered the disk."

"What disk?" She tried to act innocent.

"Let's not play this game." He glanced over at the pile on the dolly. "You're not planning a trip to the laundry at this time of night. What's underneath the towels and linen?"

He took a step toward the dolly.

"No!" Her voice rang out with authority.

She was going to have to kill him. The thought constricted her throat and brought tears to her eyes. She cared more for Arturo than she could ever admit, even to herself.

His voice softened with regret. "We're not going to have that private talk about our feelings, are we?"

She shook her head. "No."

He extended his open hands to her. "I had hoped I would not find you here, had hoped that you were not here for the disk. What are you? CIA? FBI? Or are you working for someone on the other side of the law?"

She didn't bother to answer. It was best to keep him guessing. "Who sent you?" she asked.

"Desperation brings me here." His beautiful eyes burned into hers. "I need that disk, *querida*. My brother's life depends on it. I will use it to save his life, then I will return it to your government."

She faced him squarely. "I don't have any disk, but I can help you find what you're looking for."

He took a step toward her. "Then I'll look in that little black pouch you're wearing first. What do you say?"

"No." She gathered herself, preparing to fight.

"I'll make it fun for both of us. You'll like it. I promise."

She shook her head and took a half step back. "No, Arturo," she ordered. "Don't touch me."

Jaw hardening, he moved toward her like a panther stalking its prey. "Then, do your best to stop me. I'm going to get that disk or die trying."

She took a quick breath, dancing back on the

balls of her feet, away from Bodega and the car. Arturo Bodega was among the best in the facility at hand-to-hand combat. She briefly considered drawing her gun and ending the confrontation, but suppressed the thought. If they shot and killed each other, neither would get the code.

Blocking the hand that threatened to close on her arm, she threw the first punch, a solid right to his shoulder.

"Good one, *querida*." His body absorbed the shock and he kept coming. He unleashed a flurry of calculated punches to her chin, chest and midsection.

Blocking all of them with skill, she still felt the impact of the blows on her forearms. Bodega hit hard. Gritting her teeth she held up under the assault, adrenaline muffling most of the pain. But she could not continue this way and win.

With a sudden change in tempo and style he landed a fist on her chin. Her head rocked back and she briefly saw a shower of stars.

"I don't want to hurt you," he muttered, his voice determined. "Must you be so stubborn?"

"Yes." With deadly precision fueled by throbbing pain, she lifted her right leg and caught him with a brutal front kick to the forehead. "Do *you* have to be so stubborn?"

His head snapped back and he stumbled momentarily. "See what you do to me?"

"Give up," she ordered, advancing with a series of side kicks aimed at knocking him flat on his back.

Blocking them with effort, he responded with lightning-fast sidekicks, uppercuts and roundhouse punches.

She backed up, blocking and fighting with all her heart. He had her. She was going to lose.

Reaching out suddenly, he grabbed her and whirled her into his arms, imprisoning her.

"Huhhh!" Fighting him, she twisted and turned, trying to move her feet.

"You're exciting me, *querida*." He spoke close to her ear. "Now, where is the disk? On your person? Will you make the search enjoyable for both of us?"

Rocking against him with what minute amount of movement he allowed, she tried to stomp on his instep, and failed. Then she remembered a technique she'd learned long ago.

She stopped fighting him. Bonelessly she let herself slide out of his arms and down to the cement. As he hunched forward she grabbed his arms and flipped him over her head. Bodega crashed to the ground headfirst.

The sound of his body hitting the cement sickened her. She rushed forward, encouraged that he was not convulsing. He wasn't moving, either. Deep in her heart she knew that it wasn't a trick. She bent over him, feeling for a pulse. He had an erratic one.

His lids fluttered and ink-filled eyes, glazed with pain, peered at her. "Tears for me, *querida*?"

She nodded, not quite ready to speak. There was a good chance that he would be permanently paralyzed. Her fingers smoothed the hair back from his face in a nervous yet caressing gesture.

"I surrender. I'm all yours. The only problem is that I can't move."

"You should have walked away," she said, angry that he had pushed things so far. Their friendship, the warm thing that sometimes sizzled between them, wasn't supposed to end like this.

His voice lowered. "Give me the disk."

Leaning over him, she breathed in his scent of lime and musk and pressed a kiss to his soft lips. "I can't. Maybe I can help you save your brother—"

"I saw you with *him* at the lab. You got him out of there in a space suit."

She gazed at him with amazement, regret and a touch of guilt. Heat rushed to her face and vibrated along the surface of her skin. He'd seen her with Nick and never let on.

"That is...was my husband," she admitted.

"Was?" His brows went up.

"The divorce isn't final," she admitted, not wanting to tell him the rest.

"So you're choosing him?"

"I don't know what's going to happen, but I chose him a long time ago," she answered, realization dawning. "I've been fighting it because... we've been through a bad time."

His lids fell for a moment. When they lifted, she saw acute hurt and disappointment in their depths.

"Don't try to contact me, *querida*. I wish you luck and all the love you deserve."

Reese nodded and pressed another kiss to his lips. "Hang on. I'll send an ambulance, just as soon as I'm out of here."

Seeing Bodega on the ground like that and knowing that she'd put him there weighed on her conscious and tore at her heart. If she could have taken him out of the facility with her and dropped him at an emergency room, she would have.

Standing, she retrieved one of the blankets

from the pile on the cart and covered him. Then she used what was left of her adrenaline rush to leverage Barkley's body and maneuver him into the trunk of her car. Covering him with all the sheets and towels, but ensuring that air would reach his lungs, Reese closed the trunk.

As she prepared to leave, Bodega lay conscious, but still unable to move. His face and his goodbye dominated her thoughts as she drove to the front gate, prepared to accelerate through the checkpoint or shoot her way out if necessary.

As she got closer, she saw four FBI buses and two CIA vans blocking the entrance to the camp. She stopped the car and got out, flashing her CIA identification.

The joint FBI–CIA team checked her story with Flaherty, then let her go. She had them send an ambulance for Bodega, but kept silent about Barkley. Then she was on her way.

Arturo remained on her mind as she drove the dark, deserted highway. Memories of their fight played over and over in her thoughts. No lights shone in the wooded areas along the highway and there were no open gas stations or restaurants, so she kept driving.

Five miles down the road she pulled over and made sure Barkley was still breathing. Afterward, she sat in the car, gripping the steering wheel tightly, unable to let go. She'd been through hell, yet the most difficult part of her journey awaited her. She rested her forehead against the leather-covered plastic. In her heart she wished she could wake up from the nightmare that had become her life.

Finally pulling herself together, Reese drove the rest of the way to the extraction point. She boarded the agency plane waiting for her three miles west of the freeway and sank into one of the seats, glad to give up control for a little while. Her head throbbed and she felt weak.

"Can I get you anything?" The motherly looking attendant stood at her elbow with a tray filled with sandwiches, snacks, pain relievers, water, ice, ginger ale and tequila.

Flaherty thought of everything. Reese turned away from the tequila and opted for a corned beef sandwich, soda and the pain reliever.

Two medics got Barkley from the trunk on a stretcher and brought him on the plane. In the rear, they went to work on him, talking to each other. The other attendant took Reese's keys and left to dispose of her car.

Closing her eyes, she let the sound of the air-conditioning lull her to sleep.

* * *

Flaherty was waiting for her back at CIA head-quarters in Langley, his blond hair in disarray and his steel-gray eyes almost black. "Reese, good work," he said, taking her hand and squeezing it. "You've really come through for us and we're going to do the same for you. We've got a medical team working on Barkley and getting him ready for interrogation."

She rested her forehead on his shoulder, not quite ready to hear the answers to the questions firing off in her head.

Patting her shoulder, he urged her to a chair at the table where several analysts were already seated. "Tell us everything that happened since you left the lab in Guatemala."

This was what she had been expecting. Flaherty poured her a glass of water, set the video recorder and instructed her to begin. She stopped to answer several questions.

It was nearly five in the morning when they finished the debriefing. Reese's body ached. She was so exhausted that she'd caught herself dozing off a couple of times. Still, she appreciated Flaherty doing her the favor of calling the team together to get the debriefing done as soon as possible.

"I've got to see Nick," she told Flaherty as soon as the others had left.

"You've had a difficult night and you're dead on your feet," he said, not meeting her eyes. "Rest for a while."

She felt as if she'd run a hundred miles and, as soon as she closed on the finish line, they snatched it away. She'd never seen Flaherty act like this. Was there a reason other than concern? Reese grabbed his arm.

"Tell me Nick is alive!" she demanded.

Flaherty took her hand. "He's alive, Reese, and doing better than expected, but you heard the MO on this virus. It devastates the body. We have a team of doctors working on him, recording everything—"

"He's not an experiment!" she cut in sharply, ready to battle Flaherty and the world if necessary. "You've got to save him. Evan, we need a miracle."

"Reese, we're trying our best to help him!" he snapped back, "He's in quarantine, but he's conscious and as comfortable as we can make him. The doctors have all the virus information we could find at Harwell Middlehouse Biotech and they've been going through it."

"What about the lab scientist working the cure?"

Flaherty shook his head. "Ballinger wasn't among the people we rescued and we didn't find his body."

Reese's quick intake of breath came perilously close to a sob. Acid burned her stomach as she tried to swallow past the dryness in her throat. "I've got to see Nick."

This time Flaherty didn't argue. He made a few calls, arguing with the people on the other end and throwing his weight around. He drove her to hospital himself.

Entering the sterile walls of the private wing of the hospital where they quarantined contagious patients, Reese breathed in the blended odors of alcohol and disinfectant. The nurse gave her a form to fill out. The abject pity on the woman's plain face fed the fear growing inside of Reese.

Reese dropped her head in her hands, despair absorbing the little energy she had left. She couldn't give up hope. Evan Flaherty put an arm around her shoulders. He didn't say a word.

Sitting up with her arms folded across her midsection, she opened her eyes. Then she set to work filling out the form.

Minutes later, following the nurse, she felt appreciative. They entered a room where there was a conference table stacked with papers, notebooks and a computer, four captain's chairs and an observation window. Nick's life signs on another display beeped noisily.

"I'm sorry," the nurse said, glancing at the empty chairs, "but the doctors just left to get a few hours' sleep. You can see how your husband is doing on the monitors, and when they get back, you can get suited up and go in under supervision."

Reese went to the bank of monitors, her heart in her throat. Nick lay in a hospital bed, eyes closed, wearing only a pair of hospital pajama bottoms. Sweat beaded and ran on his face and chest. On one of the monitors she got a close up of his face, his usually smooth, beautiful skin marred with a red rash.

"I want to talk to him," she demanded in a rusty voice that forced its way past her constricted throat.

"He wouldn't be able to talk to you. He wouldn't even know you were here," the nurse said flatly. "He's had a severe headache and a lot of muscle pain, so we've kept him medicated."

Crossing her arms in front of her, she stared at the monitors, wishing she could do something to help Nick. The symptoms she'd heard about from Dr. Reynolds at Barkley's briefing were imprinted on her mind. Nick already had the early symptoms. Reynolds had said that within a couple of days, symptoms progress to vomiting, diarrhea, abdominal pain, sore throat, rash and chest pain. The disease attacked internal organs and the ability of blood to clot. Specifically, the organs in the body liquefied.

Her chest was so tight it threatened to explode. Blinking, she couldn't hold back the tide of hot tears. The last thing that Reynolds had said about the virus and its victims was the most damning for Nick. All victims died within three to four days.

She had to do something. She racked her brain, trying to come up with a plan.

Flaherty pressed a wad of tissues into her hand. "Reese, go home, get a few hours' sleep. You've had a hell of night and you're dead on your feet. You're no good to anyone like this."

Planting her feet, she said sternly, "I'm not leaving till I talk to Nick." After all they'd been through, she needed him to know that she'd come back and was standing by him. She needed him to know how much she loved him and that she still cared. With the chaos at the lab, she never made things clear. She couldn't live with the thought that Nick might die still believing that she wanted to be rid of him.

As if he'd read her thoughts, Flaherty turned to her and said, "He knows that you love him, so don't worry about that. I talked with him earlier, before it got bad, and he told me that you two had a chance to talk before you parted."

The throbbing in her head eased. Reaching out, she took Flaherty's hand and squeezed it. "Thanks Evan. I still want to stay here with Nick. If I went home, I couldn't sleep knowing he was here like this."

"I'll stay with you for a while." He took one of the nearby seats.

He looked about as exhausted as she did, and she knew he was a busy man. She didn't want to keep him away from Barkley's interrogation or his time at home. "No. I'd appreciate the thought, but I'd rather wait alone."

When Flaherty was gone and the nurse returned to her station, Reese scooted one of the chairs up to the observation window and settled in. She watched Nick, taking in his every movement and correlating it with the beeping sounds coming from the monitors. Gradually, reluctantly, she fell asleep.

The murmur of conversation awakened her hours later, her body cramped and aching. Pry-ing her scratchy lids open, she watched the interplay of conversation between the four doctors assigned to Nick. The youngest was tall, thin and boyish looking. The two balding, middle-aged doctors were considering his statements, but interpreted everything in light of their own theories. The fourth and oldest was a silver-haired man who spoke of similar viruses and the techniques used for those.

When they saw that she was awake, they introduced themselves. The youngest had published a controversial thesis on the Ebola and similar viruses. The silver-haired doctor, Dr. Meyers, had held many positions as an expert at the Center for Disease Control. The other two doctors were leaders in the field of virology from the National Institutes of Health. Talking to them, asking questions, she knew that Nick was in good hands. Now all she needed was a miracle.

An odd feeling of déjà vu assailed Reese as she suited up in something like what she'd worn at the Viper lab. She hated the suit, but knew it was necessary to protect her from the virus. Dr. Meyers lectured her on the things she could and couldn't do in Nick's hospital room. Then he took a seat at the observation window to supervise the visit.

Going through an entry area with a chemical shower to sterilize everything that came out of Nick's room, Reese opened the inner door and went in.

The unmoving figure in the bed was turned away from the entrance as Reese approached. She dreaded what she would see, and yet she kept walking. Was he wasting away? Would he even be able to talk to her? As she neared the bed, the figure in the hospital bed turned. She stifled a gasp at the sight of Nick's eyes. The whites were bloodred.

Chapter 15

Reese stood by Nick's hospital bed. She had promised herself that she wouldn't cry in front of him, but it was hard to stop the tears from flowing when she saw what the virus was doing to her proud and handsome husband. In addition to the bright-red whites of his eyes, his entire body looked swollen. She forced her throat to work, her mouth forming his name. It came out on a whisper.

"Reese." His deep, familiar voice welcomed her. "Sweetheart, I didn't think I would get to see you again." He extended a hand.

Coming closer, she put her gloved hand in his. "You know I can't stay away from you, Nick, no matter how hard I try."

The last part of her statement had a little too much truth for both of them. She flinched, looking away and wishing she'd kept her mouth shut. He gripped her hand more tightly.

When she lifted her head to meet his gaze, he was calmer than he had any right to be. Had he made peace with the certainty that he would be dead in a few days?

He used the tone of voice that usually soothed her. "It's okay, Reese. The only thing that matters is that we're together now."

Within the suit she leaned the helmet against his face. It was the closest she would get to a kiss. "I love you. I love you, Nick."

"You are the only woman I've ever loved, Ree. Before you came along I didn't understand. I thought it was all about not being lonely and taking care of my physical needs. I was just playing the game. You showed me real, deep love and you will always have my heart."

Heartfelt emotion welled inside her, filling her so she couldn't speak. Swallowing hard she listened to the raspy sound of his breathing.

"Last night I heard that you were bringing

back the code—and Barkley, too," he remarked, shifting smoothly on the bed to give her room to sit. "Babe, you're the best. You are so good at the undercover stuff. I knew you'd get the code—but Barkley? I was sure he was a dead man."

"I wanted to kill him, punish him for what happened to Riley," she admitted, dropping down beside him so that their shoulders touched. "But you know how I feel about life, any life. It would have been an execution. So I acted out my fantasy and made him believe that I was going to kill him. That's how I found out about the embassy survivors. There's a chance that Riley could still be alive. Can you believe that?"

He tilted his head. "Yes, I believe it. I've prayed for that and a lot of other things." His gaze warmed and his mouth turned up at the corners. "We're together, aren't we?"

She didn't know if this moment, brought about by his illness, really counted in the scheme of things, but it *had* brought them together. "Yes." She ran a gloved hand down his arm. "I wish I could kiss you and show you how much I love you."

"I think I'd die a happy man," he quipped with a chuckle. "How do you think I got through all those months in that rebel camp? I relived all the highlights of the times we made love—like the time we did it in the cargo hold of a 747, the time we managed it in the ocean while we waited for the search-and-rescue team, or the time you were working undercover as Gallegos's girlfriend and I rappelled up the face of the cliff and into your room to find you naked…. Yeah, the real thing would probably send me on my way for good."

Reese shifted uncomfortably on the bed. His words had jogged a lot of her steamiest memories, too. Her skin felt hot and sensitive inside the suit, and she felt a pull in the pit of her stomach. She also felt the heat of embarrassment in her face. The medical staff could hear every word they said.

Using a gloved hand to cover the portion of the helmet over her eyes, she said, "Okay, Nick, baby, you've still got it. Can we talk about something else now?"

He considered her quietly, then said, "Let's talk about the service for me. I've made a list of the songs I want played and—"

"No." Feeling like she was being backed into a corner, Reese cut him off. "I—I can't deal with that right now. I don't know what I'm going to do, how I'm going to let you go…"

He gazed at her steadily, his brows going up.

"Let? Sweetheart, no one asked for your permission, mine either. If I'd been shot and killed, it would be over already. This time is a bonus and we've got to live it to the fullest. If I weren't contagious, I'd take you around the world. I'd spend every minute of it with you, on you, in you and around you." He squeezed her hand and didn't let go.

The strength of his love touched her heart and warmed her inside and out.

When it was time to go, he lay back on the pillows, the tension visibly easing from his body. "Love you," he whispered.

"Love you, too." The words felt strange on her tongue after all they'd been through, and yet they came straight from her heart. She smoothed his forehead and thick hair in a gloved caress. "I'll see you later."

Her steps were slow and reluctant as she left Nick's room. Deep inside she worried that she might not make it back before the virus took him. She went through the chemical shower and removed the suit in the next area. In the room outside, Nick's doctors sat at the table going through stacks of records and papers taken from Harwell Middlehouse Biotech. They were talking to Flaherty.

"We each have our own individual theories and insights on how best to proceed," Dr. Meyers explained. "But studies and information about this virus by Dr. Ballinger would be invaluable."

Her hands clenched into fists. *Ballinger.* She matched glances with Flaherty.

"Reese, we need to talk," Flaherty said.

She ran her fingers through the dry, brittle mess of her hair. "Did our 'friend' tell you everything you wanted to know?"

With a brief nod, he strode toward one of the small family waiting rooms and held the door for Reese. "We got a lot out of Barkley last night. It was enough to send a team into Rwanda early this morning. We have high hopes for rescuing the survivors from the embassy bombing."

"Me, too, Evan." She dropped her head into her hands, massaging the tightness in her forehead. "I've been praying that Riley will be among the survivors, but the way my luck has been running, I'm a dangerous person to love."

"Just hang in there," he advised. "I've never known you to give up on anything."

"I'm not giving up." Her teeth sank into her bottom lip. "I just wish there was something I could do. I feel so helpless. When I'm in there with Nick, his death seems like a foregone conclusion and I can't accept that."

"If Nick had been okay, I would have given you a chance to be on the team that went to Rwanda," he confided.

She thanked him and then requested a briefing on Viper and where they might have hidden Ballinger. The mask that settled over Flaherty's face spoke volumes. He was readying a team to track down Ballinger.

"You can't cut me out of this," she insisted. "I need to help Nick and I'm one of your best."

"You're also physically drained from completing a grueling mission and emotionally drained because of Nick and Riley."

Confidence steeled her voice. "I can handle it. You know I can."

"One slip and we could lose everything."

"That's why I have to be there," she insisted. "I'm willing to prove my fitness for duty."

Warmth and concern flickered in his eyes. "I'll get you an appointment with Dr. Cunningham. You get her okay, and you're in."

Nodding gratefully, despite the fact that he'd successfully maneuvered her into seeing the shrink, she accepted his offer to let his driver drop her off at home. She still wore the clothes in which she'd fought Bodega, and she felt grungy. She needed to freshen up and try to get enough sleep to match wits with Dr. Cunningham.

At home Reese showered and changed into fresh clothes. With Nick's things scattered about, it felt as if he'd just left. Most unnerving was the journal she found on their bed.

Her eyes zeroed in on the words *counselor* and *therapy* and then a dozen or more sentences about his feelings for her, his regrets about the mission in South America and his failure to reach her. He'd actually written about his feelings.

Gripping the edges of the book, she fought waves of guilt, fear, frustration and anger. She wrestled with the urge to scream. She pried her hands open. The journal slipped from her fingers to bounce back on the bed.

She drew a long, shaky breath as she stared at the journal. Words repeated in her head until she found herself whispering them. "I can't take any more. I can't take any more." Then she backed out of the room and went to lie down on the couch.

It didn't surprise her when Flaherty got her in for a late-afternoon appointment with the shrink. Reese squirmed her way through questions about her relationship with Nick and her feelings for Riley. She owned up to the loathing she felt for Barkley. Cunningham even managed to pry loose the facts of Reese's relationship with Bodega and her distress over their fight.

"You've been through a lot in the past year," Dr. Cunningham told her as the session drew to a close. "You're a strong woman, Reese, but you've got to give yourself time to heal and permission to do it. You can't keep holding everything inside. Let it go. You'll be happier for it."

Afterward, she made Reese talk about insurance, plans, and the things she would have to do if the agency didn't get the cure for Nick. Reese didn't like the things they discussed, but when all was done, Dr. Cunningham gave Reese the okay for Flaherty's new mission.

Back at the hospital, she suited up to spend more time with Nick, but he was still out from the medication. He lay on the bed, breathing harshly, occasionally tossing and turning fitfully or moaning softly. He was unaware of her presence.

After a while she went out to sit with his doctors. As soon as she entered the room, the conversation ceased. That got her attention. She glanced at each of them with the distinct feeling that something negative had transpired.

"How is Nick doing?" she asked.

They all looked at one another, and the unpleasant task of filling her in fell to Dr. Meyers. He indicated a chair.

"We've been giving him painkillers and injections of rNAPC2, recombinant nematode anticoagulant protein c2, a new treatment being used to treat the Ebola virus. It has slowed the effects of the Rage virus, but it cannot cure him. However, each day Nick survives, his chances for recovery improve. What we are really doing is treating the symptoms and buying time for Nick's immune system to respond."

The words weighed her down. Everything depended on Nick's immune system kicking in—and what kind of shape was it in? He'd been sick with dysentery and some bug when he got back from Colombia.

She asked his doctors if those illnesses could have weakened his immune system enough to affect his ability to recover from the Rage virus.

The youngest doctor, Larsen, told her that anything affecting Nick's immune system would have an impact. He quickly added that Nick was doing better than expected. The only issue now was that they'd gone through all the papers from the lab and found nothing on the Rage virus. The additional information could save Nick's life.

Hunched forward, she massaged the tight muscles in her neck and shoulders. She declined their offer of a prescription for a muscle relaxant and tranquilizer. Gazing up at the monitors, she focused on Nick's face. Sweat beaded his forehead, but he enjoyed the peace of a deep sleep.

The time she and Nick had left was so precious. Was she right to be trying to pull off a miracle instead of spending the rest of it at his side?

The devastating consequences loomed ahead, but Reese had always been a fighter. She couldn't blindly accept defeat. She'd fought her way onto the team that was going after the cure. She wouldn't come back without it.

Reese stood. "Keep him on the pain medication, no matter what he says. I'll be gone for a while."

She caught a taxi back to the agency. In her office she waited for the meeting that had been announced via her pager, and checked her e-mail. When the time came, she strode to the conference room full of nervous energy.

Inside the room, Evan was already at the media console and he was talking to Raven Ramone.

Raven wore designer clothing and balanced on delicate crochet-patterned heels. The tight, cream-colored cotton pants set hugged every perfect curve and the silken fall of ebony hair fell midway down her back. The delicate features of her face were exquisite. With Raven's exotic beauty, many forgot that she also had a high IQ. It never slipped Reese's mind.

Reese's lips curled at the prospect of partnering with Raven. She'd tried very hard to like and get along with Raven, but had never quite managed it. Yes, Raven and Nick had been more than partners for a while, but it all ended long before Reese entered the picture. Still, Reese had gotten weird vibes from Raven and caught her drooling over Nick more than once. She trusted Raven about as far as she could throw her.

Flaherty pulled charts from several files in his desk and file cabinet and put them next to the portable viewgraph machine on the edge of his desk. He was feeding three disks into the system when he caught sight of Reese.

"Reese, I know you've met Raven. I was thinking that you, Raven, David and Ell would make a good team to take on Viper for Ballinger and the cure."

Reese swallowed the negative feelings she had

for Raven and greeted her pleasantly. No matter how she felt personally about Raven, the woman was a damn good agent who would do anything to save Nick. The two women shook hands.

Flaherty introduced the other three members of the team, David Dallence, Ell Brown and Gary Michaels. Dave was FBI and working with the CIA under the joint CIA-FBI initiative directed by the President and Homeland Security. He was an electronics whiz. Ell was an agent who was also a licensed doctor with a specialty in virology. He'd published several papers on the subject. Gary was a computer genius. Flaherty introduced him while making cryptic comments about the new comm units.

When they'd all finished greeting one another and shaking hands, they took seats at the briefing modules and Flaherty began.

A picture of a white-haired, middle-aged man in a navy custom-made suit filled the screen. His piercing gray eyes leant an eerie impact to his expression. His mouth was a brutal slash.

"This is Paul Thiery. He's an Austrian citizen. Sources tell us that he is the undisputed head of the Viper Terrorist Group. This has been difficult to verify as the other rumored-to-be-powerful members heading the group have maintained their secret identities. Thiery has had an active hatred for the CIA every since his brother, Madsen, was killed in a CIA raid on a terrorist cell in Italy. Right now, Thiery is our best hope for retrieving the cure for the African Rage virus. He lives in a heavily guarded complex in the Canary Islands, off the coast of Spain. Thiery is scheduled to address the European Union tomorrow on offshore oil reserves and will be at the Venice Convention Center in Venice, Italy."

The rest of the briefing included photos of Thiery's fortress in the Canary Islands and of him with some of his women, and a list of terrorist activities he was suspected of masterminding. He was on the CIA watch list, but clever enough to leave no evidence of his activities.

Reese digested the information and considered ways to approach Thiery.

Flaherty's next words gave her hope as he changed the display to feature a dark-haired man of Hispanic heritage.

"This is Diego García Arroyo. He was arrested in California for involvement in the terrorist group Atalaya. In exchange for his freedom, we had him set up a meeting between Raven, Reese and Paul Thiery. Thiery does not know what you want, but he'll be receptive. You all have information packets to study on the man and the groups he's accused of helping."

With the rest of the team behind one-way glass, Flaherty had Arroyo brought in to talk face-to-face with Reese and Raven. He looked like a poor, idealistic student, but Reese and Raven quickly peeled back the facade to reveal a savvy, street-smart thug.

They spent a couple of hours feeling him out and quizzing him on Paul Thiery, his habits, the way he handled people who wanted things from him, and what to expect.

When they were done with Arroyo, Reese was ready to take on Paul Thiery. Flaherty sent her to have her old comm link replaced with a new one with a stronger encrypted signal. Even the new pickup sensors that came with it were more compact and easier to plant. Reese examined everything with delight. If Michaels had done the improvements on the comm units, she couldn't wait to see what he'd do on the mission.

The team took a private jet to Venice. During the long flight, Reese called in to Nick's doctors to check on his condition. The reality lurking behind their careful statements scared her most of all. She worried that Nick would be too far gone to benefit from the cure. Her stomach rumbled and her temples pounded with tension, but she forced down a tasteless sandwich to keep up her strength.

By the time they got to Venice, Thiery was giving his final remarks about the start of oil production and refining off the Canary Islands. An impressive figure in a gray suit, he spoke passionately about the importance of preserving his island's natural beauty.

Afterward, the rest of the team followed him at a distance while Reese and Raven checked into their hotel and prepared themselves for the meeting with Thiery at a private salsa club.

An hour later, they entered the club, dressed to fit in with the wild clothing some of the younger patrons wore and the conservative evening wear favored by others. Reese's short and daring zippered black satin suit was at the very limit of what she could comfortably wear, but she wore it with style. There was enough material in the split pencil skirt to hide her P226, but she knew Thiery would be checking for weapons and wires so they'd even left their comm units at the hotel. Raven's fuchsia-silk orchid dress emphasized her exotic looks and fit like a second skin. Dave had insisted on coming along, too, and sat at the bar in a stone-colored club suit. He felt that whether they needed it or not, they should have backup in sight. The rest of the team was in the van outside the club, listening in on their conversation.

Having given the hostess their names when they came in, Reese and Raven sat at a table immersing themselves in the club's hot salsa music and watching the people partying on the dance floor. Barely touching their drinks, they scanned the club for signs of Thiery. Adrenaline-fueled excitement buoyed Reese, making her forget that she was jet-lagged and tired.

They spotted him and his entourage in a private corner of the club. There were two exotic-looking women in his midst, but he was staring at Raven. Signaling for the hostess, he whispered something in her ear. The woman came to their table with an invitation to join him.

At the table in the corner, one of Thiery's men frisked them a little too intimately, making sure to brush their breasts with his hands. Reese spotted the bulge of weapons on almost all of them, including the women.

"How's my friend Diego?" Thiery asked, his gray eyes glittering.

"He's hanging tough," Reese answered, "but it's getting harder with all the attention we're getting these days."

"Where did you see him last?" he asked casually, but Reese sensed the tension in his posture.

"Paris." Reese met his gaze directly.

"What group are you representing?"

"Atalaya." Raven spoke this time. She let insolence creep into her tone. "How long are you going to waste time going through this charade?"

"As long as it takes." He signaled the hostess for another round of drinks.

Reese and Raven declined. Reese noted that contrary to their appearance of carrying on their own chitchat, each member of Thiery's entourage was listening intently to every word of his conversation.

"What's the name of the head of your group?" Thiery asked.

The name rolled off Reese's tongue. "Franco." She narrowed her eyes.

"And the guy before him?"

"Gilberto." Raven gave a tired sigh.

"We're almost done." Thiery looked from Reese to Raven. "Does Diego have a scar on his stomach or his ass?"

"Neither," Reese put in crisply. "The scar is somewhere more private."

"Excellent." Thiery laughed aloud. "Final question, ladies. What happened to Samad?"

Reese gathered herself to display outrage and horror. "We don't know who or why, but we found his…pieces in a box shipped home to his mother. Do you know something about that?"

"He was CIA, working undercover to expose your group and others," Thiery told her proudly. "I'm no fan of the CIA or its spies. What can I do for you ladies?"

Reese took a sip of her drink, the desire to strangle Thiery with her bare hands overwhelming. "My brother has been infected with the African Rage virus."

"And how did he manage that?"

"We acted on a tip and intercepted an infected CIA agent with a canister. The agent died, but not before infecting my brother and two others."

"Sorry for your loss," Thiery quipped in a pleasant tone, "but what do you want me to do about it?"

"There is a rumor that you have or know of a cure," Raven said.

"Maybe." His expression hardened. "What do you have to offer in return?"

"Money," Reese said quickly. "Three million dollars." It was money that had been confiscated from an operation with another terrorist group.

Thiery nodded. "I see that you value your

brother, but it is hardly enough to compensate me for all I lost in acquiring what I have."

Raven leaned forward. "So you do have the cure?"

"I have someone working on the cure. At this point we are preparing to test it on animals."

"If three million doesn't cut it, what do you want?" Reese asked, her tone hard.

Thiery smiled. "I want the plans to the Lightning Gun that were stolen from the U.S. Air Force. I'm prepared to settle for the world's largest pink diamond or a new chemical weapon. Surprise me."

He gave Reese a card. "Call me when you're ready to deal."

An edge of panic sharpened her tone. "I don't have much time. My brother is dying."

"So you'd better get started right away. Good night." With a nod, he stood and motioned to his people as he moved off. They all followed him.

Reese and Raven stared at each other. How were they going to get Thiery what he wanted?

Chapter 16

Anxious to find some way to cut a deal with Thiery, the team went back to their hotel on the edge of the convention center and put in a conference call to Flaherty for a strategy session.

"Thiery wants us to fail," Reese said in frustration.

"No, I think this is some sort of test," Raven said. "He knows that it's virtually impossible for us to get most of that stuff. I think he'll settle for less."

"But more than three million," Ell said. "What about the Lightning Gun?"

"And how would you explain getting your hands on that without tipping Thiery off that you're CIA?" Flaherty asked.

There was a momentary silence.

Gary tapped away on his keyboard. "What if we came up with some of the draft plans that were used for the final prototype of the Lightning Gun?"

"I'll look into getting copies of the draft documents the Air Force used," Flaherty promised.

"I could take the copies and alter them so that we wouldn't be giving anything critical away," Gary offered.

"Sounds like a plan," Flaherty said confidently. "I'll try to get encrypted scans of the draft plans for the Lightning Gun out to Gary ASAP. Gary, you'll print them out and work to alter the information. If all goes as planned, I'll have one of the scientists who developed the system work with you via a secure line."

Reese went over all the facts in her head, certain she'd missed something. "Where did Thiery go after the conference?" she asked.

"He stopped by the Al Buso restaurant to have a quick dinner with another man. I ran a check on the guy and he wasn't in any CIA files." Dave held up a photo of the man he'd printed off the surveillance system. "Afterward, Thiery went back to his hotel."

Reese stared at the picture, certain she'd seen that face before.

Raven stared too. "That's Haylen Clark," she said finally. "He works for Ventra, a storage company. They've got warehouses all over Europe."

"There's a good chance they're hiding Ballinger and the lab equipment in one of them," Reese said.

David Dallence stepped up to the plate. "I'm on it. I'll start with checking out everything they have in Venice and then spread out to the rest of Italy."

"I'm in too," Ell Brown said. "We can split the list."

"Go get something to eat, people," Flaherty ordered. "By the time you're done, I should be sending a compressed file of the Lightning Gun drafts to Gary."

"How's Nick doing?" Reese asked before Flaherty ended the call. She noticed that suddenly everyone got up.

Flaherty's long silence spoke volumes. "He's taken a turn for the worse," he said finally, "but so far the damage has not been permanent."

Reese forced the next words from her throat. "How long does he have?"

"A day, maybe two." Flaherty's low voice echoed in the room like a death knell.

There was a drumming in Reese's ears so loud she heard nothing else. "Whittaker out." She turned and left the room.

With her head bent and arms folded about her midsection, she walked the length of the hotel, fighting for control. By the time she joined the team in the hotel coffee shop almost an hour later, she was calm. She couldn't eat, but she managed to get down some hot chocolate.

As everyone dispersed, Reese offered to help download the files Flaherty had sent. Raven had already called around and found a place to print and copy the drawings once Gary made changes to them. It would be a tedious process, but worth every minute.

Reese and Raven dialed the number on the card. Thiery answered, but his voice had been altered with some kind of device. He was leaving no evidence behind. "You two seemed like resourceful women. I thought you'd manage something," he said. "What have you got for me?"

Reese spoke for both of them. "We're trying to get our hands on the draft plans for the Lightning Gun, and our chances look good."

"I asked for the actual plans for the Lightning

Gun," Thiery reminded her, his voice booming through the phone.

"The draft plans are nearly as complete. We can't get the actual plans."

"I didn't think you could on such short notice," he said. "I'll take the draft plans and the money in exchange for the cure."

"That's not what we agreed to," Raven said angrily.

"You could always take your business elsewhere," he said, knowing he had them. "Personally, I think a brother's life is worth much more than I'm asking. You two are getting a discount because of Diego."

Reese didn't have time to play games. "You've got a deal," she announced.

"How soon will you have the merchandise?"

In the other corner of the room, Gary looked up from the laptop and held up four fingers.

"Four hours from now."

"You're cutting it close," Thiery said. "It doesn't take long for the virus to cause permanent damage to the vital organs. If you let it get that far, no cure will bring your brother back to health."

"I'm working as fast as I can," Reese snapped. "We do the exchange in St. Mark's Square at six a.m."

When Thiery agreed to her terms, she felt her shoulders ease. She could only hope that Nick would hold on until she got back.

By four a.m. they were all tired, but half the team left for the square to get the jump on Thiery. No one believed he would come alone. They were still surprised that he'd agreed to come himself, instead of having his goons do the job.

At a quarter to six, Reese and Raven started the walk to St. Mark's. They headed toward the water and the end of the square where a granite lion stood on a column.

There was no sign of anyone this early in the morning. As the women neared the end of the square, a man with short blond hair and dressed in black stepped out from the library structure. Thiery wasn't with him. Didn't want to risk a bust, Reese knew.

She leaned down and put the folder containing the drafts on the ground. She kept the bag of money in her other hand. She saw the man in black place a stainless steel canister on the ground. Reese and Raven headed for the canister and picked it up as the man walked toward the folder.

As they read the typed instructions glued to the canister, Reese realized that she had no way to verify what it contained. She had to trust that Thiery was holding up his end of the deal.

"Now the other bag," the man in black said with a thick Austrian accent.

Reese dropped the other bag and kept walking, anxious to leave with her prize. They were nearly back to the water taxi when David and Ell's excited voices came over the comm.

"We've found Ballinger. We discovered heavy activity at one of the warehouses here in Venice and went in with Italian agents. We found Ballinger locked up in a cell. We're home free folks."

Reese said a prayer of thanks. She looked back to see if Thiery was visible and discovered that he and his companion had disappeared.

An hour and a half later, the team boarded a military airplane bound for the United States.

The Italian authorities would wait for the okay from the CIA before nabbing Thiery on kidnapping charges. Ballinger was willing to testify. On board, Reese sat with Ballinger and filled him in on Nick and what she knew of his condition.

Ballinger warned her that his cure had never been used on anything but lab rats. But Reese was undeterred. She knew that Nick would insist on any chance.

Adrenaline kept Reese alert and energetic, despite the strain of the past few days. Fastening her seat belt, she closed her eyes and prayed. *Dear God, please let this miracle work for Nick.*

Reese watched Nick on the monitors while the doctors talked strategy with Ballinger.

"How's he doing?" she asked the youngest doctor in the observation room.

He met her gaze squarely, sympathy coloring his expression. "His vitals have dropped a little, but we expected the drugs we're treating him with to have that effect. The next eight hours will be crucial for his recovery."

Taking a seat, Reese drank coffee. As much as she loved food, she couldn't imagine eating right now, no matter how much her stomach growled. It was going to be a long eight hours.

Flaherty called her on the cell phone he'd issued and insisted that she freshen up and get over to the office immediately. Arguing with him about her extenuating circumstances, she was surprised to lose the argument.

"We have the number for your cell phone," Dr. Meyers assured her when she told him. "If things get critical, we'll notify you immediately. You have my promise."

Reese grabbed a taxi to the house to shower

and change. She was angry with Flaherty for pulling her away from Nick. He'd even threatened to send a couple of agents to pick her up if she didn't show within a couple of hours.

At the agency, Flaherty's secretary expressed concern over Nick's condition and told her that Raven had left for the hospital. By the time Flaherty was ready for Reese, she had lost a lot of her positive energy. As she walked into Flaherty's office, Larry passed her on his way out. Surprised, she greeted him.

After expressing his regrets about Nick's condition, he explained that he was back from a successful mission and would talk with her after she met with Flaherty.

Reese stared after him. Something didn't quite gel in what he'd said. She couldn't put her finger on what it was. She shook off the feeling, certain that pushing the limits and sleeping on the run had fogged her brain.

"Reese? I can see you now." Flaherty's voice reached her from inside the office.

When she walked in he was sitting at his desk.

"I can't believe you made me come at a time like this," she began, closing the door behind her.

He pointed to his guest chair. "Have a seat. That's an order." When she was seated on the padded leather, he continued, his voice curiously missing some of the elements used when he laid down the law to her. "I thought you were getting near the end of your rope and needed to get out of that hospital environment, even if for a couple of hours. Nick's doctors say that the crucial time is an eight-hour period."

Senses tingling, she stared at him. "Evan, what's going on?"

"Bear with me." He folded his hands on the desk. "I also thought you needed to hear some really good news for a change."

"What?" She was starting to get irritated.

"He thought you'd want to see me," a male voice said from behind her.

Reese froze at the sound of a beloved voice she hadn't heard in months. She turned, shocked and amazed to see her brother standing behind her, a lot skinnier then she'd last seen him.

"Riley!" Jumping up from her chair, she ran into his arms. He caught her in a big hug and held her tight.

She didn't know she had any tears left, but they came, sliding down her cheeks like someone had turned on a faucet. Riley laughed at her, but he was crying, too.

"These are happy tears," Reese blubbered.

"Oh, Riley, they thought you were dead...and then Nick—"

"It's going to be okay, Ree," he assured her. "We're going to make it okay, right? 'Cause that's the way we're made."

She nodded, remembering the phrase their father had taught them.

"Does Dad know?" she asked, recalling how lonely their father had seemed when she last saw him. He'd been such an island unto himself after her mother died, that she hadn't known how to deal with him and had kept him at arm's length.

Riley nodded. "I talked to Dad while I waited for you to get here. The old man nearly had a heart attack when he heard my voice. He told me that he loved me, had always loved me and was sorry that he'd never taken enough time to say it."

"Wow." Accepting a wad of tissues from Evan, she thanked him for everything. "Do Carol and Candy know?"

Riley broke out in a wide, toothy grin. "Yeah, I talked to them. My little Candy princess asked a million and one questions and was absolutely positive that her Aunty Ree had something to do with getting her daddy back."

"That's true, too," Flaherty told him, cutting in. "Reese brought back Kevin Barkley, who had information that led us to the camp where you were imprisoned."

"I'm not surprised, but I'm grateful. My sister is one helluva woman," Riley declared.

"Will you allow Riley to come down to the hospital with me?" Reese asked, still holding on to his hand.

Regret colored Flaherty's expression. "No, Reese, I'm sorry. He has to go through debriefing. I broke the rules a little by letting him call his family and letting him see you here, but we have a number of agencies that are very interested in participating in his debriefing. I will try to move it along as fast as possible, but until it's over, he'll be our guest."

"Of course, Evan. Thank you." She hugged her brother once more and then she hugged Evan.

Flaherty awkwardly patted her back. "You and Nick have my prayers."

Riley gave her shoulder a squeeze. "Mine too. Everything will be all right sis."

Jittery excitement buoyed Reese's spirits as she drove back to the hospital in the early evening. She was turning into a manic-depressive. Wearing dark sunglasses against the bright sunlight, she had the windows open so that the warm air caressed her skin and played with her hair.

At the hospital, she found Nick's doctors seated at the table in the observation room, looking glum.

"What's happened?" she asked, determined not to let anything they said dash her hopes.

Dr. Ballinger spoke first. "His condition has deteriorated even more. He is dangerously close to permanent damage to his vital organs. Ms. Whittaker, I warned you—"

"Let's not throw in the towel yet," Reese snapped, cutting him off. "Isn't there still a chance that his immune system will kick in?"

"Yes, but we've been taking samples of his blood and it hasn't happened yet," Meyers added.

Reese faced them all with a voice laced with steel. "Get this through your heads. This treatment is going to work. I won't have negativity in here. My husband's life is involved. He's alive now because I didn't give up. I don't want you to give up on him, either."

The doctors nodded in silent agreement.

And several hours later, Reese was rewarded for all her effort. Nick's condition was starting to improve. The treatment was working.

Reese all but danced her way out of the hospital, only stopping to thank Nick's doctors profusely. Outside the hospital, the whole world seemed to be celebrating with her. Bright sunlight sparkled everywhere, the birds chirped like crazy and a warm breeze kissed her skin.

As she pulled into her driveway, she noted the white Acura MDX parked in front of the house next door. She didn't recognize it. As she closed her car door, she wondered briefly if her neighbor Cissy had switched boyfriends again.

Inside the house it took a moment for her mind to register the man sitting on her couch. When it did, she went for her pistol with lightning-fast reflexes.

"Don't shoot, *querida*. We don't want to hurt each other."

With the gun in her hand, Reese stopped to stare open-mouthed at Arturo Bodega.

Chapter 17

Reese blinked in shock. She held the pistol in her hand, but didn't bother to point it at Bodega. They both knew she wouldn't shoot. Her chest heaved and her heart pounded like a jackhammer.

"What are you doing here?"

"*Querida*, I came to take you up on your offer," he said in that smooth accented voice that oozed charm.

"You shouldn't be here, Arturo."

"Afraid your husband will come home from the hospital early?" he asked, putting a little bite into his words.

Reese did a double take. He knew an awful lot for someone who was just dropping in. Had he been spying on her? "Yes, my husband is in the hospital, and as you probably know, he won't be home soon."

"Then why must I leave so soon?"

She was starting to get angry. The voice in her head insisted that she didn't need a reason. Stuffing the pistol back into the waistband of her pants with a jerky motion, she started ticking off reasons on one hand. "Number one, because I asked you to leave. Number two, because I have neighbors and would not like Nick to hear about this visit. Number three, because I chose to stay with Nick—I made it very clear. And I don't cheat."

"At least not all the way," he added helpfully.

Reese's face got hot. She hadn't slept with Arturo and felt a little guilty about what went on, but the truth was that she had filed for divorce from Nick before she was involved with Bodega. He was simply trying to mess with her head.

"What do you want?" she asked through clenched teeth.

"Keep your skirt on, *querida*. Aren't you glad that I wasn't paralyzed for life?"

Her breath came out in a huff. "Of course I am. I was going to check on you as soon as the crisis with Nick was over."

"So I do have good timing." The charming smile was back.

She inclined her head reluctantly. "Right time, wrong place."

"Would you feel better if we went somewhere cozy and had dinner?"

"Or coffee," she added helpfully. "And yes, I would."

He flashed her an amiable smile. "I'll leave through the back door. I'm parked on the corner. You can follow me to a restaurant, agreed?"

"Agreed."

As soon as he went out the back door, she locked it behind him. Her heartbeat slowed. She knew that if he wanted to come back, he would, but locking the door made her feel in control.

She retrieved her purse from the floor, trying to come up with a plan for dealing with Bodega, but failing. Leaving through the front door, she made a quick scan of her block. There were no cars or neighbors out on the street, and no one was visible in the windows. She got into her car, backed out, and spotted the white Acura MDX speeding down the next block. Switching the car into gear, she took off.

She followed Bodega to a midsize restaurant

in the Hispanic section of town. Black lettering on the sign overhead said La Empanada.

"It's not coffee, but I'm homesick," he confided as he escorted her from her car "I haven't had *empanadas,* plantains, sancocho or rabo in some time."

Although fluent in Spanish, Reese did not recognize some of the foods he mentioned. Bodega laughed softly and promised to give her a lesson on Colombian food.

The place was warm, cozy and full of an exuberant group who made enough noise to cover Reese and Bodega's conversation. Sitting across from her, Bodega clearly enjoyed his food.

Finishing the last of her meal and washing it down with iced tea, Reese patted her lips with the napkin. "Great meal, Arturo, thanks. You successfully distracted me with food."

"It was my pleasure." Amusement lit his eyes. "And I always enjoy your company, *querida.*" The amusement faded. "Now we must talk about why I am here."

Elbows on the table, she leaned forward. "I can hardly wait."

"I told you that I needed the code to trade for my brother." At her nod, he continued. "With me injured in the hospital, Barkley missing, and nothing to simulate the code, there was no way I could pretend I had the code disk. I thought they would kill my little brother, but the one who has him needs money, so he gave me one last chance. My brother for two hundred thousand."

Reese tossed him a quizzical look. "Barkley wasn't paying me that much."

"I don't have the money," he said, his expression serious, "and I had no way to save so much. I need your help."

"I don't have two hundred thousand dollars," she said quickly, surprised that he would assume that she did.

"I ask that you help me to rescue my brother," he said, his voice pleading. "He has done nothing to deserve this treatment."

She placed both her hands on his thick fingers. "Arturo, I want to help you. You have to tell me who has your brother and where."

He sighed. "His name is Ivan Ríos. He's half Russian and has ties to the Russian Mafia and terrorist groups in South America, including Viper. He has a place in São Paolo, Brazil. It is a fortress. My brother is there."

"Why did he take your brother?"

"My brother is a child." His bottom lip stiffened and his right hand formed a fist. "He got involved with them and they discovered who I was and my work in special forces for Colombia. Ivan had heard the rumors that Barkley had gotten the U.S. defense code disk and blackmailed me into stealing them from Barkley or he would kill my brother. The code disk would have been like money from heaven for them."

She believed him. Her breath came out in a huff. "Okay. I've got to make some calls and go by the hospital. After that, I'll call you."

"This will help." He offered a white card with a number printed on it.

Driving back to the hospital after the meal, Reese knew she couldn't leave Nick in order to help Bodega, no matter how much she wanted to. But she figured the CIA would be very interested in getting this guy, Ríos. Besides, the agency owed her a favor or two.

Nick's doctors had not made their morning rounds yet. Reese had spent the entire night at the hospital. She had just sat down to drink some coffee when she saw on the monitor that Nick was awake. She suited up and walked into his room. The tender look on his face tugged at her heart.

"I had a nightmare and was worried about

you," he said, taking her gloved hand and tugging her down to sit beside him on the bed. "It was so vivid that I was afraid you weren't coming back."

"You were just being paranoid," she said gently. "I'm good at what I do."

"So there was no moment on this last mission when things could have gotten out of control?"

Briefly she closed her eyes. She'd been living on the edge for years. She was lucky to be alive. "Yes, there were a few moments like that."

"There'll always be moments like that," Nick said, scanning her face for her reaction. "And one day we won't have the reflexes or quick thinking to pull us through. You were right when you said I got a kick out of going out on a mission, but lying here after getting my butt kicked by this virus, I've decided I'm in no mood to take any more unnecessary risks. I don't want to be on the active list of agents anymore, Reese. I want to come home to you every night, and I want us to have babies."

Reese felt a wall inside her crumble. She knew Nick was serious. "I don't want to risk *us* again, either. I love you, Nick."

"Forever?"

Reese heard the uncertainty in his voice. "Forever." She squeezed his hand.

His smile touched her heart. "Good, because you were going to have a hell of a time getting rid of me."

"I thought about you and me and our baby this morning and realized that I want to do it again. There *has* to be something exciting we could do at the agency that wouldn't require us to risk our lives."

The corners of his mouth lifted. "I did mention it to Flaherty."

"And?" she asked.

"And we've got an offer to teach new recruits, if we want."

"If we *want?* Oh, Nick!" She hugged him as tightly as she could.

The jobs would provide all the excitement they would need for a long time to come.

Epilogue

The rowdy sounds of the football game punctuated with occasional groans from Riley and Nick, and lots of unrelated questions from little Candy filled the living room. Reese had just had an unexpected call from Artruro Bodega. She had thought she'd never hear from him again, not after learning several months ago that the CIA had retrieved his brother safely and caught Ivan Ríos.

Bodega had been brief, expressing what he said was much overdue thanks, and offering that if she should ever need him, she knew how to reach him.

Reese sat down to watch the game, reclining in the upholstered chair as Nick hovered over her like a mother hen.

"Let me get you something to drink," he offered. "What do you want?"

"A Long Island iced tea," she replied with a teasing glint in her eyes.

Nick took her hand and leaned forward to taste her lips. "I'll see if Carol has some *herbal* tea," he murmured. No, she would never need anything from Bodega that Nick couldn't give her, and more.

As he disappeared into the kitchen she thought about their past three months. Nick had been out of the hospital for more than a month, bulking up and regaining his strength. It was good to have him home, so good that they'd been acting like newlyweds. Except for work, they went everywhere together.

Reese knew that the new clinginess wouldn't last, because she and Nick were very independent, but they were both so happy to have each other again, it was hard to let go. To add to their excitement, they'd gotten wonderful news from Reese's doctor.

Candy chose that moment to stop pestering her dad and talk to Reese. "Aunty Ree," she called, crossing the room to stand by Reese's chair.

Reese bent down as Candy's arms came up to enfold her in a hug.

Holding her close, Reese kissed her on the cheek and tugged on her braids. "What's up, Candy? What have you been doing?"

Golden brown eyes regarded her solemnly. "I've been helping Daddy watch football and playing with my bear." Tilting her head to one side she asked, "Aunty Ree, Mama says you've got a baby coming. Where's it coming from?"

Reese smiled. It was still too early to let the word out officially, but she'd forgive Carol's excitement. "From inside of me, sugar."

"It must be awfully small."

Her smile widened. "The baby has to grow, sweetie, and it takes a long time to grow big and strong."

"I want a baby. Can I grow one, too?"

Laughter bubbled up inside Reese. "I think you'd better ask your Dad about that."

Nick came out of the kitchen with two glasses—a small one filled with chocolate milk and another with herbal iced tea. "Here you go, Candy," he said, giving her the chocolate milk. Your mother says you can drink it at the coffee table over there." He gave Reese the iced tea. "How do you feel?"

Reese met his gaze with love. "Perfect."

The doorbell rang and Riley went to answer. When he opened the door, his dad stood on the doorstep, looking tentative.

"Dad!" Riley and his dad embraced.

The older man released Riley with tears in his eyes. "I've been wanting to come by for a long time, but I wasn't sure of my welcome, so when Carol told me you were all here…"

"You're always welcome, Dad," Riley assured him.

"At my house, too," Reese said from her chair. She stood and met her dad halfway across the room in an enveloping hug. "It's been a long time, Dad."

"Too long," he muttered.

"Grandpa, do I get a hug too?" Candy asked.

"Of course you do, baby." Releasing Reese, he lifted Candy into his arms.

"Nice to see you again, Mr. Blackstone," Nick said, shaking his father-in-law's free hand.

"I could say the same," the older man replied with a raised brow. "I see she decided to keep you after all."

Reese laughed. "Yeah, Nick's a keeper."

At that moment, Carol came out of the kitchen to join in the fun of the moment.

Watching everyone, Reese thought about her dreams of having a family and realized she'd made that dream a reality.

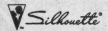

If you enjoyed what you just read,
then we've got an offer you can't resist!

Take 2 bestselling love stories FREE!

Plus get a FREE surprise gift!

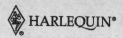

**Bestselling fantasy author Mercedes Lackey
turns traditional fairy tales on their heads
in the land of the Five Hundred Kingdoms.**

Elena, a Cinderella in the making, gets an
unexpected chance to be a Fairy Godmother. But being a
Fairy Godmother is hard work and she gets into trouble by
changing a prince who is destined to save the kingdom,
into a donkey—but he really deserved it!

Can she get things right and save the kingdom?
Or will her stubborn desire to teach this ass
of a prince a lesson get in the way?

LUNA™

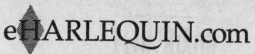

Silhouette®

BOMBSHELL™

COMING NEXT MONTH

#17 HER KIND OF TROUBLE—Evelyn Vaughn
The Grail Keepers
Modern-day grail keeper Maggi Sanger couldn't pass up the chance to embark on an expedition to Egypt to search for another legendary grail. But she'd hardly arrived before trouble found her. Crime lords, sabotage and old enemies dogged her, and at every turn, the investigation led her straight back to a very familiar man....

#18 PURSUED—Catherine Mann
Athena Force
Shaken by a dear friend's death, air force pilot Josie Lockworth hadn't been performing at her best lately. But when her latest project crashed and burned, she knew someone was trying to sabotage her career. With her boss on her case and an unsettling investigator watching her every move, she had to find out who, before her life made the hit list.

#19 KNOCKOUT—Erica Orloff
When her father was falsely imprisoned, Jackie Rooney took over his brutal business training prizefighters. Her top fighter had the chance to win a competition until Jackie received a tip that the fight was fixed and the mob was after her. Could she prove her father's innocence, save his business and escape the mob? It was all in a day's work....

#20 IDENTITY CRISIS—Kate Donovan
Kristie Hennessey was a master of disguise, but she made her living off profiling criminals, not getting involved with cases. Until an assignment turned her into an undercover agent working with a mysterious operative she knew only by his sexy phone voice. When the secretive man became a suspect, she didn't know if he was a friend, or the enemy....

SBCNM1004